ON THE INTIMACY OF LIES

Naveen K. Agarwal

This is a work of fiction. Names, personalities, places, and circumstances are either the creations of the author's mind or are exploited fictitiously. Any likeness to a real person, alive or dead, or to events or locales is purely coincidental.

First edition 2026

ISBN: 978-93-5692-139-9

Published by Naveen K. Agarwal, India

Made in India

For The Reader

For those who know that truth is not always presented but assembled through remembrance and omission, through records, judgments, and silence.

For those who understand that what is preserved is often shaped as much by power as by fact.

For readers who listen in half-light, who attend not only to what is said but also to what is deliberately left unsaid, who notice what remains after explanations are withheld, and who recognize that meaning often survives not in clarity but in absence.

May these pages offer not comfort, but recognition: a quiet, unsettling awareness of how stories endure, how they are carried forward, and what it costs personally and collectively to live alongside them without easy resolution.

This book grew over years rather than months, shaped as much by waiting as by writing, by restraint as by intention. Along the way, personal, cultural, and accidental influences helped it find its form. I am grateful to my family and friends for their patience, their trust, and the space they allowed when the work demanded time, silence, and more than words could easily justify.

I thank those who stood by during the long process of thinking, revising, and refining through uncertainty, return, and repetition. Your steady presence, often quiet and unremarked, mattered more than you know.

I am also indebted to the writers, filmmakers, and storytellers whose work sharpened my sense of suspense, structure, and misdirection, especially those who understood that silence often carries the greatest weight and that what is withheld can speak more forcefully than what is revealed.

And finally, I thank you, the reader, especially those who read attentively, who resist haste, and who allow ambiguity to remain unresolved.

This book exists fully only when read with care, with patience, with tolerance for uncertainty, and with respect for quiet.

With gratitude for your curiosity and your attention, this book is dedicated to **YOU**.

Table Of Contents

Part I

Arrival

01 - The Night That Didn't End

Some evenings resonate longer than the impact.

The car slammed into the tree with a sound strangely subdued for the force it carried—a dull compression, metal folding inward, followed by a quiet that arrived too soon, as if the fog itself had absorbed the noise.

Naina Talwar continued seated long after the engine died. Her hands lingered on the steering wheel beyond what was required, fingers curled around something that no longer reacted.

She sensed the trembling instantly.

Not pain.

Persistence.

The problem was holding on after the time for gripping had passed.

She released her hold carefully, one finger at a time, in a manner she had once been taught in another life—in chambers where control mattered more than comfort, where education arrived disguised as calm.

The dashboard clock flickered once, adjusted itself, and remained running.

That knowledge frightened her more than the collision.

The problem was holding on after the time for gripping had passed. Machines usually recognized disruption.

This one was determined to continue, to record time as if nothing of significance had occurred.

She did not cry out.

No echo followed the collision.

No delayed recognition.

Only the quiet arrival of meaning, settling where chaos might have been.

When she went out onto the road, the cold hit her immediately, efficient and impersonal, detecting hurt without sympathy.

The fog moved closer, flattening distance.

The road behind her was already fading, reduced to a remembrance without borders.

She checked herself quickly: arms, legs, and ribs.

Everything was answered.

Survival, which she achieved, often felt unstable.

Like authority that may be removed without cause.

She lingered longer than needed. Listening for sounds that did not arrive.

No engines. No voices.

The darkness offered nothing back, not even comfort.

Then she noticed the lights.

They were distant, low, and distorted by fog—not illumination, but habitation.

Too warm to be industrial.

Too fixed to belong to passing autos.

They suggested patience rather than urgency.

Waiting beside the car now felt like a decision, one that might harden into permanence.

Naina turned toward the lights.

The road dropped progressively downward before curving out of sight.

Gravel shifted beneath her shoes.

Her sleeves were dusted with dirt from the impact.

She noticed and did not brush them clean, as if cleanliness no longer applied.

As she progressed, the lights gathered into the silhouette of a large, isolated villa, set slightly apart from the road, as though distance had been chosen deliberately.

Its windows sparkled through the fog, patiently watching, untroubled by her approach.

It was New Year's Eve, 1997.

The date arrived without ceremony, like a letter slipped under a door.

She would later wonder why it had seemed important even then, why the night seemed already marked.

She approached the gate without hearing it open.

Only as her fingers closed around the lock did she realize she had not looked back at the automobile.

She did not.

02 - A Room Meant To Be Seen

The gate bore a name, etched discreetly into stone and half obscured by creeper vines, easy to miss until one stood close enough to read it. - **RIYA THAPAR**. The letters were delicate and finely etched, the font meant to express longevity rather than display.

Naina halted when she saw it. Not because the name surprised her, but because recognition arrived before context. She knew the name. Everyone did. The stillness that followed was brief but sincere.

Turning back was still imaginable. So she was pretending she hadn't noticed. She stood long enough to understand that observation itself had now become part of the pattern.

The gate opened without protest. No one answered her knock at the villa door. That information registered only after she was already inside.

The living room was immaculate in a way that resisted comfort. Furniture placed not for use but for observation. Surfaces devoid of excess, aligned into quiet uniformity. Even the lighting seemed calibrated—bright enough to expose, soft enough to forgive. Her footfall sounded invasive. She became aware of her breathing, shallow and erratic, as if the place needed a different rhythm than her body could deliver.

Riya Thapar reclined on the couch. For a moment, Naina's thinking resisted the conclusion her sight had already formed. She saw the crimson dress first—how meticulously it held its shape, how it resisted wrinkling—before knowing that the color did not fully belong to the material.

Blood had soaked into the cushions beneath Riya's head, spreading outward with a slowness that suggested time had already done its work. Her face was still. Too still. The diamonds around her neck collected the light and returned it without judgment.

Naina felt something unfamiliar—not shock, but adjustment. Nothing else in the room was disturbed. No smashed glass. No fallen furniture. No hint of urgency. The absence of chaos felt deliberate. As if the room had been instructed to be silent.

That was when she saw the man standing nearby—Ronnie Grewal. He did not recognize her approaching. He stood back, hands loosely clasped, attitude neutral, like someone waiting for a procedure to begin. Naina knew, with amazing clarity, that the incident on the road had not taken her to safety. It had delivered her to Riya Thapar's villa.

03 - Controlled Voices

Ashima Roy strolled down the stairs without haste.

Her outfit was unremarkable by design: pants, a simple shirt, and nothing that attracted attention or signified authority of the space.

Her hair was forced back tightly, as if imprisonment were a moral choice.

She paused on the final step and took in the room without reacting.

Her gaze moved first to Ronnie.

Then to the body.

Only then did she speak.

"You've destroyed everything."

The sentence dropped without volume or fury.

It sounded like a choice already decided.

Ronnie reacted immediately.

"I didn't do anything. I was upstairs. She was dead when I came down."

Ashima listened as if testing alignment rather than truth. When he finished, she turned her head slightly and spotted Naina standing at the doorway.

Her tone shifted, not softened but formalized.

"Who is she?"

Naina felt the room recalibrate around the question. Whatever she was going to say would not exist on its own.

It would be used.

04 - An Eyewitness Was Born

Naina introduced herself with care.

She recounted the accident.

The road.

The fog.

She decided to approach the residence rather than wait.

Each statement was factual.

Adjustable.

As she spoke, she became aware that accuracy alone would not protect her.

What mattered was not whether her story was true, but whether it could be accommodated, taken in without effort, and made to fit perfectly among competing perspectives.

She had learned this years ago, in rooms where inquiry was framed sweetly and replies were rehashed without noticing.

In such contexts, quiet had never represented absence.

It had symbolized choice.

She adjusted instinctively, not the facts, but their weight.

Ronnie listened with studied stillness.

He neither interrupted nor encouraged.

His attention appeared measured, as if he were assessing how much space her narrative consumed and if it was beyond allowance.

"This doesn't have to become complicated," he said gently.

Ashima had been observing Naina from the minute she entered the room.

Not her face, but her stillness—the way in which she neither hastens to fill it nor steps aside from it either.

It signified someone unfamiliar with being managed but capable of learning how management worked when it arrived.

"You didn't come here looking for trouble," Ashima commented.

Her tone was dull, almost mechanical. "That matters."

Naina did not respond.

She was beginning to realize that emotions, here, were not always clear, that rejection and assent may register without words.

Ronnie lowered his voice slightly, not out of concealment, but out of habit.

"People who cooperate in situations like this," he said, "usually don't regret it."

The sentence carried no emphasis.

It was not persuasion.

It seemed like a rule, one that existed independently of him, previously established elsewhere.

Ashima remarked, as if describing a technical difficulty, "Things settle. Names don't get dragged.

Stories don't grow teeth."

Naina registered the wording quickly.

Things settle.

It conveyed more than relief.

It suggested duration.

A universe in which this moment would not stretch beyond its allotted boundaries, would not acquire edges sharp enough to cut.

She gazed once at the body on the couch, then back at Ashima.

The action was small, almost instinctual, but it registered. Everything did.

"I don't want to be involved," she continued.

"No one does," Ashima said.

"Involvement isn't always a choice."

The stillness that followed was not tense.

It was evaluative, as if an option were being judged for weight rather than quality.

Naina nodded once.

Not agreement. Recognition.

From that moment on, the blackness reshaped itself around her.

She was no longer only a stranger who had arrived by accident.

She had been noticed.

Placed.

Nothing had been promised.

But something had been established.

05 - The First Arrangement

With Naina's hesitant recognition established, the room shifted from reaction to work.

Ashima moved first.

She did not state what needed to be done. She began doing it.

She drew up the sleeves of her top and proceeded to the side table, removing objects just long enough to clean beneath them, returning everything to its place with precise accuracy. Her motions were efficient, almost practiced, as if this job had been in her thoughts long before this night.

Ronnie studied her for a moment, then followed.

"Every surface," Ashima commented quietly.

"Anything that can remember touch."

Ronnie nodded and got a rag.

He worked slowly, avoiding the couch, avoiding the body. Panic, he knew, left traces. Control did not.

"The time has to move," Ashima continued. "Not much. Enough to distort the sequence."

She stared at Naina, neither asking nor commanding.

"Your accident helps," she said. "It gives us margin."

The remark hit forcefully. Not safe. Space. For no reason she could later explain, Naina considered refusing, saying nothing, stepping back, and leaving the room entirely.

The thought passed as quickly as it came.

When Ashima looked at her, Naina was already nodding.

"The vault," Ronnie said. "We make it look like theft."

"Yes," Ashima replied. "A mess but selective. Nothing personal. No rage."

But, surprisingly, the vault was empty.

No cash. No will. No valuable assets. Nothing.

Ronnie frowned.

"Just yesterday," Ronnie said, "I saw Riya putting cash in the vault. It's not here now."

Ashima cut in sharply. "This is not the time to think about that."

They worked without further discussion.

Drawers were shoved open, contents disturbed just enough to suggest intrusion.

Jewelry cases were toppled, their contents left behind.

The objective was not loss but illumination.

Ashima paused once, surveying the room. "No broken glass," she noted.

"Forced entry makes noise. We need something quieter."

Ronnie thought this, then nodded. "The side passage."

"That will do," she said.

Throughout all that transpired, Naina remained where she was.

No one instructed her to help.

Her existence had already been accounted for. That, she recognized, was instruction enough.

When the room had been transformed enough, Ashima stepped back.

"It will read as opportunistic," she commented.

"A robbery that went wrong. People understand that."

Ronnie picked up the phone. He did not call promptly. He fixed his posture first, straightened his expression, and inhaled once, deep and measured.

Then he called the cops.

"My wife..."

His voice broke at precisely the proper place.

"My wife has been murdered."

There was a pause on the line.

He repeated the name more clearly this time.

"Riya Thapar."

That name required no clarification.

When the talk finished, the house felt different.

Quieter.

As if it were already being remembered rather than occupied.

Ashima glanced once at the clock.

"From this point on," she added, "we repeat. Nothing new."

Naina recognized that whatever had just been done could no longer be undone.

The setup was complete.

06 - The First Fracture

After surfaces had been wiped and after instructions had been delivered and accepted, the house remembered precisely what it had been taught. Ashima returned to her room alone. It was smaller than the rest of the villa, practical rather than expressive. A bed made too neatly. A desk cleared of personal items. The kind of space meant to absorb residents without evidence. She shut the door behind her. Not fast. Control did not require speed.

She sat for several seconds, listening. Downstairs, voices moved fluently, purposefully—the sound of systems interacting. The pulse of repetition was already rising. Only then did she enter the bathroom.

She locked the door. The mirror returned her image without modification: eyes alert, jaw held too tightly, breath arriving in shallow corrections. She placed her hands on the porcelain edge of the sink. The surface was freezing. Reliable.

This was the part she had postponed. She had anticipated fear. She was prepared for guilt. What she had not prepared for was the calm that followed completion—the moment when nothing further was required, and the future arrived already shaped.

Statements. Depositions. Repetition.

She saw it clearly: years of restricting herself before language fully developed. Of stopping mid-sentence. Of knowing which version belonged to which room. Survival was not escape but maintenance.

Her stomach tightened. A sound escaped her—not a sob, not a scream, but a sudden intake of air that fractured into something close to both. She covered her mouth, as if the walls were listening. She did not collapse.

Instead, she straightened. Her reflection settled again. Almost.

From beyond the villa, a siren rose—distant at first, then unmistakable. It did not wait for permission. It declared itself with authority.

The agreement was no longer private.

She inhaled again, deeper this time, and adjusted her stance. By the time she unlocked the door, control had returned. Not fully. But enough. No one below would notice the difference. Only Ashima knew what it had cost.

By the time the police arrived, the essential decisions had already been made. What remained was not truth, but endurance.

Part II

The Official Story

07 - A Crime Made Predictable

Because it was a high-profile case, the police responded fast. By the time Inspector Daulat Talpade arrived, the house had already decided what it was going to be.

His uniform was immaculate, pressed into certainty itself. He did not pause beside the body and did not linger where grief or shock might demand attention. He did not ask for timelines, or who had arrived first, or how long anyone had stood still. Instead, he asked only those questions meant to narrow the story rather than expand it.

Statements were given. Each was received without expression and slotted neatly into a narrative he appeared intent on completing.

When he pulled Ronnie aside, his voice lowered, not in anger, but with the weary precision of a man managing inventory rather than lives.

He adjusted his cap, a habitual motion, as though order might be restored by straightening what was already aligned.

"This was supposed to be simple," Daulat said. "A predictable problem. A manageable one."

"Sir, I," Ronnie began.

Daulat raised a hand. "Don't explain. Explanations leave traces."

His gaze shifted briefly toward the living room, where the forensic team was beginning to assemble equipment.

"By morning," he continued, "this will be a robbery gone wrong. Forced entry. Panic. Blunt trauma. A tragic but familiar story."

A faint tightening stirred behind his eyes. He ignored it.

Ronnie swallowed. "And... us?"

Daulat's eyes hardened. "You and Ashima were victims of circumstances." He paused just long enough for the words to settle. "That's the kind that survives the paperwork."

Silence followed not long after, but it was heavy enough to carry its cost.

"You remember our arrangement," Daulat added quietly. "Except now, the risk has doubled."

Ronnie nodded immediately. "I'll arrange it."

Only then did Daulat straighten his cap again.

The agreement was complete. It was neither written nor recorded, yet trusted all the same.

A constable approached, notebook in hand.

"There were no disturbance calls, sir," he said. "No neighbors reported noise."

Ronnie answered without hesitation.

"The rooms are soundproofed," he said. "We renovated a few days ago."

Daulat glanced up. "All of them?"

"Bedrooms. Living areas. Study." Ronnie's shoulders lifted faintly. "Riya valued privacy."

Daulat wrote it down.

Soundproofing explained the silence. It allowed the night to remain undisturbed.

"There were threats," the constable added, flipping a page. "Typed notes. Received over the last month."

Daulat was unimpressed. "Everyone visible receives threats."

"Same wording each time," the constable said. "No signature."

Daulat nodded once. "Add it to the file. Atmosphere. Not motive."

The file accepted it easily.

Silence. Threats. Renovations.

Each detail explained the next without ever asking why they had appeared together.

It was the night of December 31st. While the city outside prepared to celebrate, the villa remained hushed, tense with impatience.

Dr. Rosie Panicker arrived with her forensic team soon afterward. She worked according to her own rhythm.

She studied the room carefully, as if listening to it rather than seeing it.

Her team moved with practiced efficiency—photographs taken, measurements logged, evidence sealed—but her attention kept drifting back to the corner table.

"Was anything moved before we arrived?" she asked.

"No, ma'am," Constable Gopinath Patil replied. "At least... nothing obvious."

She nodded, unconvinced.

"There were two vases here," she said after a moment.

No one answered.

"One remains," she continued. "Cleaned thoroughly. The other is missing."

She crouched and traced the edge of the table with her gloved fingers. A small imperfection marred the wood, nearly invisible unless one knew how to look.

For a moment, she hesitated. Her hand hovered above the surface, poised between documentation and dismissal.

She was aware of Inspector Daulat behind her, of the weight of his silence, and of how easily a detail could become a nuisance instead of evidence.

She straightened, reached for her camera, and then lowered it again.

The pause lasted barely a breath, but she experienced it as a decision.

Not yet, she told herself. Later. When the room is emptier.

"A blow strong enough to fracture the skull," she said instead, her voice even, "requires weight, balance, and proximity."

Her eyes lifted, meeting Daulat's without flinching.

"If the injury caused death," she added, "then the weapon remained here long enough to be cleaned, or it was important enough to be removed."

Silence settled over the room.

Dr. Rosie exhaled slowly. She knew what she was doing. Or rather, what she was postponing.

"This isn't absence," she concluded. "This is extraction."

Inspector Daulat Talpade already knew how the night would end.

The house had been prepared. The witnesses were cooperative. The absence of noise had been explained before it was questioned.

Fear, he had learned long ago, lost its power when categorized correctly.

There had been a case years earlier, small and forgettable by public standards. A petty thief with poor timing and worse luck. The man could not pay what was expected of him. He pleaded instead, explaining circumstances when money was demanded.

Daulat had not been interested in explanations.

What followed was never written down. Only understood.

The man returned quieter. Compliant. Grateful for restraint that had not been shown.

Months later, Daulat's wife left. No note. No warning.

She left with the one person Daulat had assumed would never dare approach him again.

The department learned quickly. Jokes became careful, laughter quieter, and doors closed before voices carried too far. No one addressed it directly. They valued their postings. Their safety.

Daulat did not retaliate. He corrected.

From that point onward, he stopped believing in attachment altogether. Desire, he learned, was easiest satisfied when power removed negotiation. Consent was a courtesy extended to equals.

He had never mistaken women for equals.

The department understood this.

Files shifted. Complaints dissolved. Transfers were adjusted. Daulat remained untouched, not because nothing had happened, but because nothing had been recorded correctly.

He straightened his cap and surveyed the villa.

"This case will close quickly," he said. "Let's not complicate it."

Footsteps sounded from the corridor.

Unhurried. Deliberate.

A man entered the room without announcement. He did not look at the body first. Instead, his gaze moved across the people's postures, silences, and the shape of authority in the room.

Inspector Daulat stiffened almost imperceptibly.

Victor Banerjee had arrived.

He wore a black jacket, unobtrusive by design, the sort that belonged equally in offices and courtrooms. The cuffs were neat, though worn thin with use.

And unlike everyone else in the villa that night, he had no interest in the version of the story that was easiest to complete.

No one saw Victor as he entered the home.

There was no announcement, no interruption, just a person standing in the doorway, taking in the space as if it were a solved equation to be pandemonium.

He did not gaze at the corpse first. He stared at the crowd.

His hair was meticulously pushed back, already thinning in a way that showed attentiveness rather than contempt.

08 - What Was Removed

At Ronnie's, hands clasped too hard. At Ashima's stillness too trained. Inspector Daulat was already scripting the ending in his head. Only then did Victor turn toward Riya.

He noted the tilt of her head, the location of the incision, and the odd cleanliness of the nearby region. His eyes wandered, inexorably, to the corner table.

"One vase," he said softly. The room stilled.

Dr. Rosie turned toward him. Their eyes met, recognition burning rapidly between professionals who spoke the same language.

"Yes," she answered. "One is missing."

She glanced at the evidence tray on the wall. Her pen lingered over the introductory notes. For a fraction of a second, she pondered leaving the phrase "decorative item" vague, perhaps "displaced," or that sort of wording that fostered cooperation, minimized friction, and kept reports from becoming battlegrounds. She had done it before. Not lies. Just tenderness.

Dr. Rosie's pen touched the paper. Then she stopped. One transparent, solid glass vase, commensurate with blunt-force dimensions, is missing from the scene.

Removal appears deliberate. She inhaled slowly, as if releasing something she hadn't known she was keeping. Only then did she stare back at Victor.

Victor nodded, as if it verified something he had felt all along. He did not adjust his clothes. He rarely did. Control, for him, had already been settled earlier in the day.

"Then someone didn't just kill her," he said. "Someone planned what we wouldn't be permitted to see."

Inspector Daulat cleared his throat. "And you are?" Victor finally gazed at him. "Someone who doesn't close cases," he remarked. "I open them."

Inspector Daulat Talpade stepped out onto the balcony, the night air thick with fog and cigarette smoke. He had hardly lit one when he sensed someone behind him.

"You're closing it too fast." Daulat did not turn around.

"Crime scenes don't wait for philosophers." Victor paused a few paces away. He did not enter Daulat's region. He didn't need to.

"A robbery-murder," Victor said firmly. "No forced entry worth mentioning. A cleaned living room. A missing weapon that happens to suit the height, weight, and reach needed to inflict that injury."

Daulat expelled smoke.

"Coincidences occur."

"Not like this." That made Daulat turn.

"Listen carefully," Daulat added, his tone measured. "This case is sensitive. Powerful people are watching. If you complicate things, you won't be appreciated for it." Victor met his stare without blinking.

"You're not worried about complications," he added. "You're concerned about delays."

Daulat's jaw clenched. "By morning," Victor went on, "your paperwork will say the body was discovered after a robbery, the suspects were cooperative, and the evidence was inconclusive but sufficient."

His garments remained unchanged, as if purpose had reached beyond consciousness.

"And if it does?" Daulat asked. "What then?"

"Then you'll have committed yourself," Victor remarked.

"Because if the weapon turns up later—and it always does—you won't be able to argue you didn't hurry the conclusion." Daulat hurled ash over the railing.

"You think you're the first man to threaten me with a procedure?"

Victor shook his head.

“I’m not threatening you,” Victor said. “I’m documenting you.”

Daulat examined him very attentively now. "Who asked you to come here?"

"No one," Victor said. "That’s usually how it starts." A brief quiet followed.

"You should walk away." Daulat observed finally. "This city rewards silence."

Victor turned to depart. "I'm not here for rewards," he said. "I’m here because someone thought erasing a vase would erase the truth."

He paused. Just once.

"And Inspector," he replied, "when this case collapses, it won’t be because of evidence. It’ll be because you sought to sell the end before reading the middle."

Victor moved back inside, leaving Daulat alone with the fog, the cigarette burning down between his fingers. He pounded it out harder than needed.

09 - Professional Distance

Dr. Rosie approached the crime scene the way she normally did, with emotional detachment passing as discipline.

Her coat was immaculate, buttoned firmly despite the warmth. Her hair was secured tightly, leaving nothing free enough to distract. Trauma, she believed, left patterns—not just on bodies, but on places, relationships, and lives. Her mission was to discover such patterns before emotion contaminated them.

She recognized the obvious first: disordered furnishings, strained symmetry, and the immaculate disarray of a situation striving to express itself too well. Someone had wanted a story to be believed.

She removed her gloves with painstaking care, tucking them inside before setting them aside, as if captivity extended beyond the person on the table. She wrote it down.

Victor arrived without introducing himself. He smelled oddly like antiseptic and paper offices rather than people. He always did. Even during their marriage, he entered rooms as if already expected, already justified.

She felt him before she saw him, a tightening in her chest,

first annoyance, then something colder. She stepped away, positioning herself behind a structural column, assuring herself this was not avoidance. It was control.

Surgeons were trained early on how to compartmentalize. So were pathologists. They collided, nevertheless. Not physically. Something subtler.

"You're here," Victor said.

It was not a question.

"Yes." Her voice sounded calm. She noticed it too. Emotional neutrality often passed for recuperation.

"You're with forensics?" he asked.

"I was asked to assess the scene independently." There it was. Independently. The word lingered. She saw how rapidly he recalculated, how instinctively he searched for angles rather than meaning. That had always been his skill. And his flaw.

Years ago, he had explained carefully why a lie had been necessary. Rosie had understood immediately and realized rationality was no longer the issue. The trouble was how easily he rationalized.

Back in the present, Victor gazed toward the living room. "It looks staged."

"Yes," she said. "So do most things meant to hide violence."

She regretted the severity in her tone but did not soften it.

She touched her sleeve once, the gesture tiny and habitual, then stilled her hands.

He turned back to her. "Are you including marriages?"

The question landed harder than he expected. Or perhaps exactly as expected.

She recalled standing over a patient who had died hours earlier, the cause listed as cardiac arrest. She had thought then, That's not why he died. That was how it ended.

She met Victor's eyes. "Marriages rarely fail from a single cause," she said. "They accumulate damage. Neglect. Rationalizations. Small, recurring injuries."

He absorbed that quietly. Too quietly. She wondered, not for the first time, whether Victor believed his narratives or merely found them useful.

Around them, the investigation progressed. Officers moved through the space, touching nothing that mattered, missing everything that did. Rosie closed her notebook.

"Whoever did this," she said, "wanted the death to appear simple. Accidental. Understandable."

Victor nodded. "That's usually what convinces people."

"Yes," she replied. "And it's usually wrong."

She recalled their last argument. No shouting. No accusations. Just papers scattered across a table and the unspoken knowledge that both had fled long before the divorce was formalized.

In the hallway, Victor adjusted his waist. "You always did see things before anyone else."

"And you always decided what to do with that information," she said.

Silence followed. This time, Victor looked away. She passed him, her shoulder brushing his arm.

The contact was brief, involuntary, and too familiar. She felt the reflex to pause, to explain, to diagnose. Instead, she kept walking.

In the next room, Rosie jotted one final note: Emotional concealment mirrors forensic hiding. Both rely on disinformation. Both fail under persistent inspection.

Behind her, Victor stood alone, watching with a narrowing gaze. He had always managed difficulty by forcing evidence into coherence. The thought unsettled him now. He wondered whether the same instinct that had sustained his marriage had also taught him how to survive incomplete realities.

Neither of them spoke again.

But the murder had already begun to resemble something else entirely.

10 - Paperwork And Profit

The lawyer arrived while the villa remained under procedural lockdown.

Vikram Singh introduced himself politely, then waited, neither rushed nor hesitant, until acknowledgment permitted him to proceed. Only then did he place a sealed folder on the table. He did not sit until invited to do so.

When he did, he aligned the folder precisely with the table's edge, as though orientation itself were an act of respect.

He wore a light-colored suit that wrinkled easily, the kind meant for offices rather than scenes of consequence. Nothing about him suggested endurance. He looked like someone accustomed to accessing places that were not his and leaving without residue.

"I'm here regarding Ms. Riya Thapar's life insurance policy and her revised will," he said calmly.

"The coverage totals one hundred million dollars. My responsibility is to determine whether any listed beneficiary could have been complicit in the circumstances surrounding her death."

The investigating officer nodded. "You mentioned documentation."

Vikram slid the folder forward.

"This is a certified photocopy of Ms. Thapar's amended will," he said. "It was revised last month. She instructed me to submit it on the first of January."

"And instead," the officer said, "you're here today."

"Yes. I learned of her death this morning and came immediately."

The seal was broken. Pages were turned. The room grew quiet in the way it did when figures replaced speculation.

A month earlier, Riya Thapar had sat alone in her study, the drapes drawn against the afternoon light. The document lay open before her, its margins dense with neat, precise annotations.

She signed slowly, deliberately, as if the act itself needed to register.

"This version is final," she said. "Make sure it's treated that way."

"There's still time to reconsider," Vikram had said carefully.

She shook her head.

"There isn't."

He hesitated. "The insurance nominations remain unchanged."

"That's intentional," she replied. "They don't need to match."

Back in the present, the officer scanned the pages again.

"This revision removes several major heirs."

"That's correct," Vikram said.

"And yet the insurance beneficiaries remain the same."

"Yes."

"Why the separation?"

"No explanation was provided," Vikram said. "Only urgency."

Footsteps approached.

Ronnie Grewal entered the room.

He paused just long enough to straighten his jacket before moving closer. His attention went immediately to the folder.

"This is the will?" he asked.

Inspector Daulat looked up. "You seem eager, Mr. Grewal."

Ronnie smiled thinly. "I'm surprised. Riya never mentioned altering anything."

"It was revised last month," the officer said.

Ronnie frowned. "That doesn't make sense."

A bead of sweat surfaced near his temple. He brushed it away quickly, as though irritation rather than fear had produced it.

The silence that followed was brief but exact.

Victor, standing near the doorway, noticed it.

The officer turned another page. "Under this version, certain individuals no longer inherit anything."

Ronnie leaned forward. "Then who does?"

"That information isn't being disclosed at this stage," the officer replied.

Ronnie straightened.

"However," the officer continued, "the insurance documentation tells a different story."

"Insurance paperwork often lags," Ronnie said too quickly.

Vikram looked up for the first time. His voice remained even. "In this case, the option to revise was discussed."

Ronnie turned sharply. "And she declined?"

"Yes," Vikram said. "Explicitly."

The contradiction settled into the room without resistance.

Inspector Daulat intervened smoothly. "For now, we'll treat this as an administrative inconsistency. There's no need to complicate matters prematurely."

The officer considered him, then nodded. Ronnie's shoulders eased just slightly. Victor saw that too.

Vikram remained seated, hands folded loosely on the table. He did not look at Ronnie again. His attention had already moved elsewhere, toward the process, toward the speed with which friction was being erased.

The prescription records were brief but consistent. Sedatives. Anti-anxiety medication. Adjusted twice in three months.

“She wasn’t sleeping,” Ronnie said. “Stress.”

“Hallucinations?” the officer asked.

Ronnie paused only long enough to be measured.

“She complained of noises. Crying. But nothing concrete.”

The dosage increases were recorded without commentary.

Medication fit cleanly into the narrative forming on paper: wealth, pressure, instability.

No one asked what the drugs were meant to silence.

“You were Ms. Thapar’s legal advisor?” Victor asked.

“I work with Desai & Associates,” Vikram replied.

“Insurance and liability,” Victor said. “That requires a law degree.”

“Yes.”

Victor waited.

“I qualified three years ago,” Vikram added. “The firm Mr. Desai assumed liability after a restructuring.”

“Before that?” Victor asked.

"Before that," Vikram said, "others carried it."

Victor held his gaze a moment longer than necessary.

Inspector Daulat closed the file. "This will be reviewed."

Vikram stood. He adjusted nothing. He collected nothing. The folder remained on the table.

"As requested," he said.

As the discussion ended, Vikram stepped back, allowing the room to settle into its prior alignment. He did not reinsert himself. He had already placed what needed placing.

In the hallway, Victor watched him leave.

There was nothing remarkable about Vikram Singh. No visible grief. No urgency. No claim.

Yet one detail refused to release its grip.

Vikram had never asked who stood to gain more from the insurance than from the will.

He already knew.

Truth, Victor understood, did not always arrive searching. Sometimes, it arrived fully informed.

11 - The House Without Staff

The police began recording testimony one person at a time, using a method that sounded impartial but followed its own logic.

Doors were closed. Recorders were switched on.

Names were written, then rewritten, until they fit neatly within the borders of the form.

Ronnie Grewal was advised to contact the domestic staff. He complied at once.

He stood beside a policeman while making the calls, holding his phone slightly away from his body, the volume raised just enough for the officer to hear. His voice remained steady, kind, apologetic, and almost regretful.

One by one, the calls went unanswered.

No cook.

No driver.

No gardener.

No watchman.

The officers exchanged looks—not alarmed, but unsettled. In a house of that scale, absence itself became explanatory.

"This estate requires round-the-clock staff," one of them remarked, scanning the room. "Where were they all last night?"

Ronnie answered without hesitation. "Riya was upset. She told everyone to leave."

"All of them?" the officer asked.

"Yes."

The word settled into the room without resistance.

They moved through the villa's next bedrooms, service corridors, and staff quarters. The spaces were orderly but not abandoned. Beds were made too tightly. Uniforms were folded, not discarded. Personal items were arranged with care.

It did not look like panic.

It looked like instruction.

In the staff quarters, a register lay open on a table near the door. Names were listed. Attendance recorded. In the margin, a note had been written neatly:

All personnel dismissed for the evening. Instructions from Madam.

The handwriting was controlled. Unemotional.

Inspector Daulat read it briefly, then handed it back.

"How many people work here?" he asked.

A number was given.

"And are all of them accounted for?"

There was a pause.

Someone counted quietly. After a moment, one of the older helpers spoke.

"Sir... Himmat Singh is not here."

Daulat looked up. "Who is he?"

"The driver," the man replied. "Caretaker also. Oldest staff member."

"How long has he worked here?"

"Many years, sir. Before most of us."

"And where is he now?"

No one answered.

They went to Himmat Singh's room last.

The door was locked. The policeman broke it cleanly.

Inside, the space was sparse in a way that suggested purpose rather than haste. The cupboard was empty. The bedding was neatly folded. A pair of worn shoes missing from their usual place. His personal papers were gone.

Inspector Daulat stood in the doorway taking it in.

"So," he said. "He leaves when everyone else is dismissed. He takes his belongings. He doesn't return."

He turned to the officer beside him. "That isn't absence. That's departure."

The phrase was written down.

Himmat Singh's name moved swiftly from the staff register to the suspect column. No explanation was required.

Orders followed. Railway stations. Bus depots. Airports. Border checkpoints. His description was circulated. An old personnel photograph was retrieved—creased, faded, and adequate.

Inspector Ghosh spoke into the radio. "Arrest immediately upon sighting."

No one questioned it.

One of the helpers spoke again, reluctantly this time.

"Madam didn't like the windows after sunset."

"Why?" an officer asked.

"She said someone was standing far away," the man replied. "Watching."

"Who?"

The hesitation was brief. "Sometimes she said it was Sahib."

"Mr. Thapar?"

"Yes."

The explanation softened as it was recorded.

Grief.

Medication.

Stress.

Across December, every staff member described Himmat Singh in the same way: calm, attentive, and protective. He checked the locks. Walked the boundary. Reassured her when she grew frightened.

No one found that unusual.

As the investigation continued, a pattern emerged.

Riya Thapar had been furious. That much was settled quickly. She had been demanding, volatile, and dismissive.

The dismissal of the staff fit cleanly into that portrait. Their absence afterward required no further inquiry. The narrative clarified more than was necessary.

One of the officers glanced up from his notes. "It's convenient," he remarked, without accusation. "An empty house. A missing caretaker."

Inspector Daulat nodded. "Criminals often take advantage of convenience."

Victor, standing a few steps away, remained silent. He was looking at the register again at the handwriting, the timing, and the lack of dissent.

"People don't usually flee from houses they've protected for decades," he said at last.

Daulat regarded him steadily. "People do many things when they're afraid."

Victor did not respond.

Later, when the remaining staff were released after questioning, their statements aligned without effort.

Riya had been enraged. She had ordered them out.

Himmat Singh had looked uneasy but obeyed. No one had seen him since.

The version held.

As dusk settled over the villa once more, Vikram Singh passed by the servant quarters.

He did not stop.

He did not look inside.

There was nothing left there that needed attention.

Himmat Singh had already been filed.

12 - Prior Alignment

Naina had once sat at a workplace where nothing personal was allowed to stay. Not on desktops. Not in files. Not in memory.

The guy opposite from her had spoken softly, almost sheepishly, explaining that a mistake had happened.

That being in the wrong location at the wrong time had garnered excessive attention.

Attention, if mismanaged, tends to multiply.

"We are not asking you to lie," he had stated. "Only to be precise."

Precision, she discovered, did not imply truth. It implied utility.

She watched as her statement was reorganized, not by altering events, but by dispersing them. Cause softened. Sequence shifted.

Emphasis moved until the version on paper no longer matched what she recalled but contradicted nothing demonstrable.

When she hesitated, the guy grinned.

"This version survives," he remarked. "The other one creates work."

She signed without protest.

There were no threats. No raised voices.

And yet she departed with the strong impression that something irreversible had been determined without her input, that a line had been crossed silently and would not be crossed back.

Standing there at Riya Thapar's villa, Naina knew the rhythm instantly.

This was not a risk. This was protocol. And protocol, she understood, did not need consent, only compliance.

Part III

Maintenance

13 - Rehearsed Anger

The staff were questioned individually, yet their answers arrived pre-aligned.

Different rooms.

Different chairs.

The same cadence.

They began, almost instinctively, with Riya's anger, as if starting there simplified everything that followed.

She had been furious that day. Louder than usual. Unreasonable. Demanding.

The word "angry" surfaced repeatedly, offered without emphasis, as though it described a permanent quality rather than a condition that required confirmation.

Each sentence reinforced the next. Madam Riya had ordered everyone to leave the estate. She did not want staff present that evening.

The instruction had come through Isha Diwan, as it usually did. No one questioned it. No one stayed behind.

When asked if this was unusual, heads shook gently.

"Madam was often like this."

The repetition did not feel rehearsed so much as practiced. These were not lies assembled in haste, but habits formed over years—what one said when authority demanded justification, when temper excused disruption, and when circumstances needed a version that could be carried without strain.

Inspector Daulat listened without interrupting.

"How many of you work here?" he asked.

A number was given.

"And everyone left?"

"Yes, sir."

A pause followed. Someone recalculated softly, the count being adjusted without acknowledgment.

"Except Himmat Singh," one of them said.

Daulat looked up. "The caretaker?"

"Yes. Driver also. Oldest staff."

"When was he last seen?"

No one knew. Or no one chose to say.

They moved to the staff quarters next.

Himmat Singh's room was locked. When the door was forced open, the space inside required no interpretation. The cupboard stood empty. The bedding was folded. Shoes were gone from their place. Papers removed.

It was not disorder. It was a departure.

Daulat paused at the doorway, already shaping a sequence.

"He leaves when the house is empty," he continued. "Takes his belongings. Doesn't return."

No one contradicted him. Silence settled where corroboration would have been unnecessary.

By the time the officers returned to the living room, Himmat Singh's absence had begun functioning as an explanation.

His name moved easily from the staff register to the suspect column—without motive, without context, and without anyone needing to acknowledge that the movement itself was a choice.

Someone asked if he had access to the house.

"He had keys," came the reply. "Knew routines. Timings."

That was sufficient.

The remaining staff were released in stages, their statements recorded, summarized, and filed. The phrasing varied, but the conclusion did not.

Riya was volatile. The house was empty. The caretaker was gone.

Across the room, Isha Diwan stood with her hands clasped at her waist. Her posture was formal, almost ceremonial, yet something in her stillness resisted the efficiency unfolding around her.

When asked whether Himmat Singh could have harmed Riya, she answered at once.

"No, sir."

Daulat studied her. "You're certain?"

"He protected this house," she said. "Like it was his own."

Daulat nodded. Certainty was unnecessary. Plausibility was sufficient, and even that could remain provisional.

It was then that the fear surfaced.

"She used to say Tina came at night," one of the maids said quietly.

Daulat looked up. "Which Tina?"

"The girl who died," she replied. "Desai Sahib's daughter."

No one corrected her.

Another staff member added, "Madam said they cried. Outside the rooms. That's why she sealed them."

Daulat considered this briefly.

"Hallucinations are common under sustained stress," he said mildly.

The words were written down.

Fear became a condition.

Soundproofing became a symptom.

"And the notes?" Daulat asked.

"Yes," the maid said. "Typed. Always the same words."

"What words?"

"You will die soon."

Silence followed.

Then the sentence was recorded.

Someone mentioned Riya's political ambitions. Her growing visibility. The threats she had received.

The idea was accepted with relief—a story large enough to absorb uncertainty without asking too many questions in return. A rival. A warning. A professional intrusion.

The earlier anger-based explanations receded, replaced by something broader, less personal.

The case expanded just enough to justify its closure.

Coffee arrived in disposable cups.

The inspector accepted his without comment. The constables did the same.

Ronnie and Ashima declined.

Dr. Rosie waved it away.

Victor took one and did not drink.

When Isha approached Naina, she handed her a cup already prepared.

"Black coffee," she said. "Less sugar."

Naina accepted it with a slight nod. She did not appear surprised. The familiarity passed without remark.

The room settled again, quieter now, more assured.

Anger had been established.

Absence had been translated into guilt.

Procedure began to outpace uncertainty, its momentum comforting to those who relied on it.

No one noticed how effortlessly it had happened.

By the time the final form was signed, the narrative no longer required witnesses.

Constable Gopinath Patil entered to report that a dog had been found lying motionless behind the bushes.

"My God," Isha said softly. "That must be Leo. Poor thing. I hope he's still alive."

No one responded.

The machinery was already moving forward.

14 - Two Versions, Neither True

Ronnie and Ashima recounted the same tale. That was the requirement.

They were questioned individually, at various hours, in rooms made to seem impartial. Chairs were arranged at equal distances from the table. Nothing lay on the surface except the statement sheets.

The recorder was turned on only after identities were validated and spelled correctly.

Inspector Ghosh performed the questioning.

Inspector Daulat stayed there, listening, acting only when necessary. Ronnie spoke first.

He reported hearing a sudden, heavy, unmistakable crash. Something powerful hitting wood or stone. But the villa's rooms were soundproof and re-interiorized just last month, and the sound reached him blurred and uncertain.

When he entered the living room, Riya was already dead. The intruder had vanished by then. His voice stayed level. He sat erect, jacket still on despite the heat, hands resting neatly on his knees. He talked in meticulous sequence, as if order itself would ensure truth.

The story was sound. Ronnie could see that immediately. What unsettled him was not its plausibility, but how little room it left him to change it later.

Daulat listened without taking notes.

Ashima came later. She reported rising voices and a fight in the living room. Sharp words were exchanged. After the noises stopped, she headed downstairs. By then, Riya was dead. The intruder had already fled.

Her hands were curled firmly in her lap. A stray strand of hair lingered against her temple. She did not move it.

Her voice kept low, controlled, and tailored to fit what had previously been said.

There was no contradiction left to correct. The printed assertions represented a single version. A disruption. A quick debate. An intruder. A corpse was found too late. Timings were modified. Language softened. Absences were converted into explanations.

Nothing published was strictly untrue, yet nothing remained untouched.

Ronnie signed instantly.

Ashima read every line. She stopped long enough for the pause to register. Then she signed.

Daulat lined the sheets with care, tapping the stack once on the desk. This was the version that would stay. The escape route was noted as undetermined but plausible. The intruder was claimed to have escaped by a corridor connecting to the main structure of the home. No forceful entrance was reported. No valuables of interest were missing. The act was regarded as exact, controlled, and disciplined.

Attention moved to the caregiver. Himmat Singh was described as someone having access to keys, procedures, and blind spots. He knew the home well. He had not been seen since that night. The coincidence was recorded.

Outside the room, Victor stood near the hallway window. He could not hear the words, but he knew the rhythm.

Ronnie's calm and composed. Ashima's internal strain. Control on one side, constraint barely holding on the other.

The case was tentatively filed as a robbery. The discrepancies were graded as minor.

Inside the room, Ashima sat alone under the fluorescent light. Her signed statement sat on the table. The ink had begun to dry. Permanent.

Ronnie entered shortly later. He spoke quietly, as if serenity itself might seal the decision. He claimed it was over. Ashima gazed at him. She wondered how many versions presently existed.

Ronnie told her just one mattered. She stated they still did not match. He reminded her they did not need to match. They merely needed to live. When he grabbed for her arm, she jerked away.

Victor stared through the glass window. He saw enough of the imbalance, the asymmetry, and the silent shift of power as dread started to manifest.

The case would not fail because of evidence. It would fail because someone will forget whatever version they were defending.

15 - When Silence Testifies

The room was smaller than the others, windowless, its air held tight. A single table. Three chairs.

Inspector Ghosh sat opposite Isha Diwan, his notepad open but untouched for several seconds longer than necessary. Outside, the corridor held its quiet assembly.

Ronnie and Ashima stood among the others, waiting. No one spoke. Even curiosity had learned to keep its voice low.

Inside, Isha spoke carefully. She repeated what had already been recorded, adhering closely to the version she understood was expected of her. Her voice remained even, neither defensive nor eager.

She described the evening as it unfolded. The times. The instructions were issued. The order in which the staff departed.

Nothing excessive. Nothing softened.

Then she added one detail.

Earlier that evening, she said, she had seen Ronnie in the pantry.

He had been working deliberately, his back to the door. Not hurried. Not furtive. She had watched him take out a small vial and add something to a bottle—the one Riya drank her scotch from.

She did not say poison. She said substance.

The word lingered between them.

Inspector Ghosh looked up. He asked why Riya would drink from a bottle kept in the pantry.

Isha explained that a fresh consignment of alcohol had arrived the previous afternoon for the New Year's celebration. Most of it was standard stock. Riya madam's bottle was different, expensive, and imported separately.

The day before, Riya had instructed her to clear the bar counter and replace all bottles with the new delivery.

Later, after the argument with Ronnie, Riya had told her to move her bottle into the living room instead.

Ghosh replied quietly that no such bottle had been found.

Isha nodded. When she returned after the police arrived, she already knew this. The bottle was missing.

When Ghosh asked why the image of Ronnie in the pantry had stayed with her, Isha answered without pause.

"Because he never goes to the pantry."

The inspector made a note.

She said she had left only because Riya madam had ordered

the staff to go. Once an instruction was given, it was not questioned. The house emptied quickly. Lights were switched off. Doors were closed.

As she was leaving, after the others had gone, she remembered hearing voices.

Ronnie speaking to Ashima.

The voices were controlled. Not raised. No longer scattered by movement.

She could not distinguish sentences. Only words.

Thief. Robbery.

They surfaced briefly, detached from context, spoken without urgency yet with intention.

She did not stop to listen. She accepted the words as they were—partial and unexplained—and left as instructed.

Inspector Ghosh recorded the information without interpretation.

When asked about Himmat Singh, her posture shifted.

"He would not do this," she said quickly.

Ghosh watched her. "You're certain?"

"He protected this house," she replied. "He treated it as his responsibility."

"But he left," another officer noted.

"Yes," Isha said. "After securing the gate. After securing the kennel."

The room fell silent.

Ghosh waited. "Then who do you think killed her?"

Isha hesitated. Composure alone was no longer enough.

She glanced toward the door—toward where Ronnie and Ashima were waiting—then lowered her eyes.

"Maybe they did," she said. "They would have their reasons."

After a pause, she added, almost apologetically, "I don't understand how rich people live."

She fell silent.

Then, without prompting, she reached into her bag and removed a folded sheet of paper.

"Madam asked me to keep this," she said.

Inspector Ghosh unfolded it.

YOU WILL DIE SOON.

Typed.

No date. No signature.

"Envelope?" he asked.

"No."

"Fingerprints?"

"None."

He nodded, already classifying it. "Typed threats usually frighten more than they act."

The note was filed under Psychological Stressors.

Isha did not speak again.

Outside the room, the change was immediate.

Quiet. Methodical. Final.

Ronnie and Ashima stood among the others. Isha emerged without looking at them.

Ashima felt it first as a tightening at the base of her neck and pressure behind her ears. She kept her gaze on the floor, following the cracks between the tiles, confining herself to that narrow geometry.

Ronnie stepped closer. The sound was small. Ordinary.

Ashima flinched, then corrected herself instantly. Her foot tapped once before she pressed it flat.

Across the corridor, Naina stood unmoving, her hands steady. That constancy unsettled Ashima more than anything Isha had said.

Ronnie leaned toward Naina, lowering his voice. "You didn't show her anything," he said. "While we were planning."

Naina did not answer at once. When she did, her tone was flat.

"I didn't see anyone."

She tightened the strap of her backpack. "For the record, this plan was yours. I was present. That's all."

She met his eyes without apology.

"Let's keep it that way," she added. "Statements have a way of correcting themselves."

Ronnie looked away. Ashima waited for him to turn back.

He did not.

Victor approached. "What's happening?"

Ronnie answered quickly, saying he had only been arranging transport for Naina.

Victor listened, then spoke evenly.

"No one is leaving."

It did not sound like authority. It sounded procedural.

"Statements are still being recorded," he said. "Until that's complete, everyone remains available."

He let the silence finish it.

"This is not a request."

The corridor complied.

Ashima's hands had gone numb. She flexed her fingers once, startled by the delay in sensation. She did not move again.

Silence did not accuse. It was confirmed. And something she had maintained for years, carefully balanced, precisely held—she understood at last it would not be allowed to return to its previous shape.

16 - Adjusting The Clock

The room was small. Windowless. A table placed there for utility rather than comfort. Two chairs, one occupied, one observing.

Naina answered the questions carefully. Not slowly. Not defensively. With the precision one uses when lifting something that could not be dropped once raised.

She had not changed clothes since the night before. Dark, unremarkable fabric chosen to disappear in places where attention lingered longer than intended.

She had learned early that neutrality passed more smoothly through institutions than emotion ever did.

When asked when she had arrived at the villa, she paused.

Only briefly—long enough.

"About twelve forty," she said.

The officer wrote it down.

The pause had not been for calculation. The number had already been chosen.

What she sensed instead was the moment itself—the instant when time, once spoken, became fixed enough to be used.

She remembered the dashboard clock clearly. The faint green glow. The second hand hesitated before beginning its slow rotation.

12:15 a.m.

The image did not waver. It remained intact. She did not correct it.

Twenty-five minutes was not much.

It could pass unnoticed.

It could be dismissed as an error.

It introduced just enough looseness into the sequence—just enough space for later actions to settle without resistance.

What unsettled her enough to show was the realization that she could no longer distinguish recall from adjustment.

The memory remained exact.

So did the alteration.

They existed side by side without conflict, neither displacing the other.

She continued.

She said that Riya was already dead when she arrived.

That portion required no revision.

She described the villa as it had appeared—orderly, quiet, and already resolved into something arranged to be understood.

She did not mention the clock again.

As the officer read her statement back to her, Naina listened closely. Not for accuracy, but for shape.

The version returned to her was clean. Plausible. Easy to move forward.

She nodded when asked.

Later, standing alone by the hallway window, she found herself repeating the pause.

Not the time.

The hesitation itself.

It occurred to her too late to be useful that she had not considered whether she might ever need those twenty-five minutes again.

The adjustment had come effortlessly.

What troubled her now was not that she had changed the record, but how little effort the change had required and how impossible it had become to identify where the original moment ended and the managed one began.

By the third week of December, the town had begun to treat repetition as routine.

Naina looked down the market road and felt a familiar sensation settle in her chest.

She had walked it before.

Recently.

The recognition passed without commentary. It did not require interpretation. It simply existed—another instance where memory arrived already aligned with expectation.

The proceedings would continue.

So would she.

The clock, once adjusted, did not demand explanation. It only required consistency.

And consistency, she had learned, was a skill sharpened by use.

17 - The First Unmanaged Moment

The bathroom door latched with a gentle, definitive click.

Ashima stood by the sink, palms braced on the porcelain, shoulders squared as if stance alone might still operate as teaching.

The mirror reflected a familiar arrangement—hair in place, expression contained—but the alignment no longer convinced her. She breathed once. Then again. The heartbeat would not settle.

She realized the difference instantly. This was not panic. Panic was unpredictable and external—something that could be addressed with effort.

There was the delay: her body arrived a trifle too late for judgments she had already made. A sound escaped her before she could fix it. Sharp. Brief. Human.

She placed her fingers to her lips, then lowered them, realizing that the sound had already occurred. It would not be taken back. She did not collapse. She lowered herself softly to the floor, back against the cabinet, knees drawn in just enough to preserve stability.

For the first time, she let the future gather without interruption. Not as danger, not abstractly, but as a sequence. Interrogations that repeated. Statements that hardened.

Control had always been something she inhabited comfortably. Now it seemed like something she would have to carry.

A knock sounded. “Ashima?” She did not answer at once. The delay registered even to her. She stood. She washed her face. Adjusted her hair. Tested her voice once beneath her breath, then again loudly. “Yes.”

When she answered the door, her stance had returned. Her expression had adjusted. The mechanics still operated. But the effort necessary to run them had altered.

As she went back into the hallway, she understood without relief, without drama, that nothing ahead would allow for repose. Control would no longer recover itself automatically.

It would take care.

Repetition.

Maintenance.

Something fundamental had been squandered.

Not broken. Expanded.

18 - A Case That Wouldn't Hold

Ashima learned of her arrest by the sound of the latch. It was not loud. Not dramatic.

Just the clear metallic affirmation of technique completing itself—a mechanism accomplishing exactly what it had been designed to do.

She sat erect. Hands folded. Posture correct.

Someone had once told her that posture was remembered while words were forgotten. She believed that. She adjusted her shoulders slightly, aligning herself within the room.

The policeman read out the charges. The words passed through her without resistance. Murder. Conspiracy. Tampering with evidence. They sounded technical. Almost abstract. Categories rather than accusations.

She focused instead on the fluorescent light above. It flickered once, then stabilized. That unsettled her more than the allegations.

A momentary failure, swiftly repaired. No record of interruption.

Ronnie stood nearby, calm and attentive. He caught her gaze and nodded. Small. Reassuring. Practiced.

"We expected this," he said. "This is transient."

Ashima nodded back. The movement cost her more than it should have. As they were led down the corridor, she noticed a delay in her body's response to instruction.

Her feet hesitated half a beat after she decided to walk. Not enough to be seen. Enough to be felt. She corrected it. Correction had always been her strength.

Meanwhile, Isha's testimony, supported by preliminary findings, had led to the arrest of Ronnie and Ashima as the primary suspects in Riya's murder.

The detention followed a formal, efficient, almost choreographed procedure yet offered no sense of closure.

The case was full on paper but hollow in substance, as if something essential had been assumed rather than secured.

Dr. Rosie and Victor recognized the same weakness. Without recovery of the murder weapon, the case would fracture under scrutiny. Circumstantial alignment could not survive extended cross-examination.

Ronnie and Ashima might still walk free. Evidence, not conjecture, would decide their fate.

The search for Himmat Singh continued in parallel. Orders were issued. Until he was found, he remained both suspect and absent—a convenient vessel for doubt.

19 - If I Forget It Correctly

VIP detainees were kept in secured rooms designed to signal safety, restraint, and discretion.

Inspector Daulat Talpade, by contrast, appeared entirely untroubled. His uniform was immaculate, every fold aligned, every button exact. The setting did not disturb him. The outcome had already been rehearsed elsewhere.

In private, he was confident the arrests would not hold. He had spoken carefully and selectively with Ronnie and Ashima about what would follow. Their release had been assured in return for a sum significant enough to warrant precision but not urgency.

The absence of the murder weapon did not concern him. It was not a flaw. It was leverage. And leverage, applied at the correct moment, carried more weight than evidence ever could.

In the holding room, Ashima sat alone. The chair was cold, rigid, and resistant to comfort. She folded her hands, then unfolded them as numbness crept in. Sensation returned slowly, as if waiting for permission.

Her thoughts did not return to Riya. Nor to the villa. Instead, her mind drifted to a file she had mislabeled years earlier—a minor clerical error. It had been corrected within minutes. Forgotten by everyone else.

Yet she remembered how long it had stayed with her afterward. The awareness of it. The residue. That memory surfaced now with disproportionate force, insistent and uninvited.

The door opened. Inspector Daulat stepped inside, his expression neutral, his tone almost considerate.

"This will not proceed as it appears," he said. "The case is weak."

Ashima nodded automatically.

"You'll be out," he continued. "But you must remain aligned."

Aligned. The word did not reassure her. It sounded procedural. Instructional. Like a correction applied too late in a process already compromised.

"Yes," she replied.

The sound of her own voice startled her. It was unnaturally steady. As though it belonged to someone trained for moments exactly like this.

Daulat observed her for a fraction longer than necessary. Then he left.

Elsewhere in the compound, near the boundary wall, evidence surfaced briefly before it could settle.

Fabric fibers had been recovered. Old. Rough. Theatrical in texture.

"Someone wanted to be seen," Victor said quietly. "From a distance."

"Costume?" a constable asked.

"Possibly."

Victor did not write it down. He had learned that not everything provable could survive procedure. Himmat Singh's name already occupied that space on the page.

Back in the holding room, Ashima sat alone again. She realized she could no longer reconstruct the night cleanly. Not emotionally. Not in sequence. The order had begun to blur, events sliding past one another without friction. The effort produced a dull pressure behind her eyes. She closed them briefly.

From somewhere unsteady, a thought surfaced clear, uninvited, and unsettling: If I forget it correctly, it will survive.

The idea frightened her more than remembering ever had. Because forgetting, she now understood, was not erasure. It was preservation performed with care. And care, once learned, was difficult to unlearn.

Part IV

Pressure

20 - Curated Truths

Ashima was questioned again late in the evening.

Same room. Same recorder. Slightly different chairs. She spotted it instantly. The chair across from her had been pushed closer. Not confrontational. Efficient. Close enough to register without provoking a remark.

The officer talked gently. His questions were unaltered.

That was the problem. Repetition, she recognized now, was not reassurance. It was pressure exerted over time. A pause too lengthy.

Ashima sensed it as a tangible delay, like a lost signal reconnecting, a system slowing before recovery.

She waited for the next inquiry, but it didn't appear.

The officer looked at the recorder. Something had altered. Not the answer, the timing. She adjusted forward, restoring her posture, centering herself via alignment.

The movement was automatic and practiced. Her spine straightened. Her shoulders settled. She put her feet flat on the floor. These were measures she trusted. They had worked previously. The words piled up wrongly now. Not contradictory or mismatched. Close enough to pass, close enough to strain. She could feel it happening.

Her body reacted before her mind: a constriction in her neck, a small tremble in her hands.

She pressed her hands flat on her thighs, pushing until feeling returned, until the trembling lessened. Silence extended.

Ashima recognized, with a rising certainty that troubled her, that stillness no longer felt neutral. It felt interrogative, as if it were waiting for her to deliver what had not been requested.

When the interrogation was completed, she was brought back to holding.

She passed Ronnie in the hallway. He grinned faintly, the expression practiced and comforting.

"You did fine," he remarked.

She nodded. But the phrase no longer mapped into something she could check. It wandered, unanchored, divorced from cause or measure.

That night, alone, she attempted to practice the statement. The words no longer came in sequence. She skipped parts without realizing, surged forward, then doubled back. Her intellect adjusted itself automatically but more slowly each time, as if drawing on a resource already drained. Alignment now needed effort. And exertion left residue.

21 - What Refused To Settle

In Dr. Rosie's forensic office, time moved differently.

Victor worked continuously. The lights never dimmed fully, and the air carried a persistent undertone of disinfectant layered with old coffee. His jacket appeared more often now, sleeves permanently creased at the elbows; he had stopped trying to smooth them.

He moved between the evidence table and the small window overlooking the service road, scanning files, witness testimonies, and timelines with mechanical focus. Autopsy photographs lay face down between sealed documents, handled with care and speed. Days blurred into nights as he pursued every lead, however weak, aware that a single ignored detail could undo everything they had built.

Across the stainless-steel desk, Dr. Rosie studied the autopsy data again—slowly this time.

Her workspace was basic and practical: no windows, only racks of labeled binders, a neatly stowed microscope, and a wall clock that ticked louder than it should have. She removed her spectacles and cleaned them once, then again, though they were already clear.

She knew the results by heart. Still, her eyes lingered in the margins—the spaces where interpretation thrived and certainty thinned. She lifted her pen.

A small alteration in language. A firmer emphasis on force or angle. Nothing untrue—only cleaner. Enough to support the prosecution without misrepresenting the findings.

She hesitated.

For a moment, she pictured the courtroom: the judge nodding, the defense faltering, the case holding. She imagined the relief it would bring, not only to the investigators but also to herself. Closure carried a logic of its own.

Then she laid the pen down.

Rosie acknowledged, without judgment, that the decision would limit what followed. The report remained unchanged. She closed the file, aware that restraint carried its own cost. Fidelity preserved her ethics, but it might weaken the case.

Outside the office, the building slept. Inside, the casing refused to.

Victor stood near the window, his reflection faint against the dark glass. His collar was open now, the jacket draped over a chair—the first concession to fatigue.

Dr. Rosie sat opposite him, file closed, her conclusions apparently settled.

"We're missing too much," Victor said quietly. "A vanished weapon. Statements that don't stand alone. Witnesses who remember just enough to protect themselves."

Rosie did not disagree. She remained upright, hands folded atop the file, as if posture itself were evidence.

"Incomplete testimony isn't accidental," she said. "It's curated."

Victor turned to her. "By someone who understands the system well enough to bend it."

"Inspector Daulat doesn't bend evidence," she replied. "He redirects it."

The ventilation hummed in the silence that followed. That was acknowledgment enough.

"And then there's Himmat Singh," Victor said.

Rosie lifted her eyes. "Yes."

"Does it make sense," he asked, "for a loyal staff member to suddenly commit something like this?"

"Loyalty doesn't erase opportunity," she said. "But it doesn't fit easily."

"Finding him might," Victor said. "If he's alive."

Rosie frowned. "You think he's a witness?"

Victor lowered his voice. "What if he saw something he wasn't meant to? What if he was an eyewitness—and he's already been killed? Ronnie is very cunning."

"But there's nobody," Rosie said.

Victor's expression didn't change. "Daulat could have disposed of it. He can do anything for money."

Rosie didn't argue.

"Daulat will find him," Victor continued. "Alive or otherwise. He always closes his loops." He hesitated. "Only then can Ronnie be saved."

"Saved," Rosie repeated—not as agreement, but as observation.

She reopened the file, the paper whispering softly.

"Forensically," she said, "there's something else that doesn't settle."

Victor waited.

"If Ronnie poisoned her, why kill her violently afterward? Why the vase?" She touched the toxicology page. "Poison offers distance. Control. Minimal traceability."

"And a quieter death," Victor said.

"Yes. Easier. Safer." She looked up. "He gains nothing from striking her—not the estate, not insurance. Violence improves nothing."

"The report confirms death at midnight," Victor said.

"That's solid," Rosie agreed. "But the cause remains difficult." She turned the file toward him. "The poison was present—enough to impair and to slow her. Not enough to kill."

"And the blunt force?"

"Severe. Multiple impacts. Consistent with the vase."

"So which killed her?"

Rosie paused. "That's the problem. The timeline converges. Midnight. Poison active. Impact delivered." She hesitated. "Separating cause from contribution becomes almost academic."

Victor exhaled. "Exactly where a defense attorney would live."

"And thrive," Rosie said.

Her fingers rested on a handwritten note she had added earlier—a conditional phrase, defensible but generous. Her pen lay beside the file. She picked it up. Then stopped.

A single line, shaped differently, could narrow the space the defense would exploit. Might preserve the truth from those who weaponized doubt.

Rosie exhaled and struck through the note—not erasing it, but marking it unmistakably. She closed the file. The sound was final.

Victor noticed her hands linger on the cover.

"The poison won't save them," she said at last.

He didn't ask.

"It didn't kill her," Rosie continued. "But it slowed her. Made her less careful."

A beat. "That is all I will say."

Victor turned back to the window, his reflection stretched thin by glass and fluorescent light.

"In court," he said, "they won't ask what happened."

Rosie nodded. "They'll ask what failed."

Silence followed. Somewhere beyond the office, a chair scraped. A door closed.

"I won't change the cause of death," she said finally. "No matter who asks."

Victor smiled—not in relief, but in acknowledgment.

22 - The First Day Of Court

Ronnie employed one of the most feared criminal lawyers in the state, Saamiya Siddiqui.

Known for eliminating cases before they reached trial, she moved fast, keen on closing the issue on the very first day of hearings.

Her renown preceded her into the courtroom, shifting its balance before she spoke a word.

Ronnie dressed in a basic shirt and slacks. He adjusted his collar once before the proceedings began, a little typical adjustment, then settled into calm.

The courtroom was already filled when Ashima was brought in. Not crowded. Ordered. Bodies arranged with purpose.

Every participant sat where the protocol asked them to be seated, their duty clearly determined before a word was uttered.

Ashima noticed this instantly. Order had always calmed her. Today, it seemed bizarre. She took her seat beside Ronnie.

The bench was narrow. Their shoulders did not touch. That, too, appeared deliberate.

Distance without enmity. Separation without accusation.

Ashima folded her hands in her lap. They did not remain stationary.

Given the public sensitivity surrounding the murder, the likelihood of evidence tampering, and claims made at the highest administrative levels, the court had authorized expedited processes in unusual situations.

Efficiency carried the weight of urgency. Urgency carried its authority.

The judge entered. Everyone rose. Everyone sat. The cadence was precise. Predictable. Good, Ashima thought. Predictability meant safety.

Saamiya Siddiqui climbed with calm dominance. Her attire was beautifully fitting, rigid in its lines. Nothing about it suggested accommodation.

She paused not to gather her thoughts but to adjust the little silver ring on her index finger, a typical motion that accompanied her silences. Only then did she speak.

"This case," she submitted, "is entirely baseless. It contains no evidential weight and depends solely on guesswork and story fabrication.

The local police have squandered precious time on a proposition unsubstantiated by evidence. By all legal measures, it's an open-and-shut case."

Her voice was unhurried and properly metered. She went slowly. Several indicators, she argued, showed that a robbery had taken place.

The vault had been brutally destroyed. Riya Thapar, intoxicated and physically unprotected, had been unable to fight assailants and had been slaughtered in the process.

The crime scene, she concluded, aligned perfectly with a robbery-homicide scenario.

Ashima listened closely. The words were familiar. She had heard variants of them before. In private rooms. In preparation. In reassurances offered quietly and convincingly. She endeavored to match them to memory. The alignment shifted. Only slightly.

Saamiya's attentiveness altered suddenly. "Why," she continued, advancing toward the prosecution table, "is this private detective, Victor, present at every step of this investigation? Who authorized him to collect evidence, question witnesses, or immerse himself in official proceedings? Under what legal mandate?"

Victor stood when authorized. He buttoned his jacket before speaking, then left it fastened longer than needed.

"If the investigating agency believes my presence at the crime scene on the night of the thirty-first of December was coincidental," he replied calmly, "they are mistaken. I received an official email from Riya Thapar a week before her death. My business has been professionally affiliated with the Thapar family for years. Ms. Thapar trusted me solely on sensitive matters."

He added that she had begged him to visit Palankhet fast, expressing significant anxiety. Before he could arrive, she was killed.

Then he unleashed information that rang throughout the courtroom.

Ronnie, he asserted, was considerably indebted after continuous losses in the stock market. gambling, and hazardous investments. A renowned spendthrift and serial womanizer, he had long cast covetous eyes on Riya's holdings. Ronnie had joined the Thapar family as an investment planner.

Over time, Riya had been emotionally tied to him, wanting a spouse who would bow to her formidable nature.

Ashima's appointment as Riya's personal secretary, Victor claimed, had also been managed by Ronnie. Riya had uncovered the whole magnitude of their deception just days before her death.

In retaliation, she assumed all professional authority,

removing her husband from office operations and keeping him out of financial decision-making. Evidence of this change, Victor argued, was demonstrated in internal emails and administrative paperwork. The purpose was unmistakable: money.

"It was the concealed intention of both Ronnie and Ashima," Victor stated, "to eliminate Riya for financial gain. These concerns were thoroughly addressed in the email she sent me." He sent a printed copy.

The judge studied it briefly.

"This printout, in isolation, holds no evidentiary value," the court remarked. "However, in conjunction with the supporting documents submitted, permission is granted for your formal inclusion in this investigation."

Victor continued. While most of the evidence looked procedurally good, the forensic analysis concerned him significantly. Certain judgments, he maintained, were irreconcilable with the physical reality of the crime.

"There are unresolved aspects," he noted. "What has been presented does not fully describe what happened to Riya Thapar. I request extra time to undertake the investigation."

Before the court could answer, the public prosecutor stood.

"This is a murder of a high-profile individual," he submitted.

"The gravity of the offense, the influence of the accused, and the continuing investigation make this an inappropriate case for release. Releasing the accused at this time would compromise justice."

He hesitated, then replied, "The police are still searching for Himmat Singh, a crucial link in the case. His version must also be heard. He may be an eyewitness."

The judge thought that through. "The absence of a key witness is noted," the court said. "The investigating agency is directed to arrest Himmat Singh at the earliest and place him before this court."

Turning back to Victor, the judge added, "Submit all tangible proof at the next hearing. Despite the fast pace of these proceedings, you are provided time until the next hearing. Use them wisely."

The court added that Naina will be called for testimony if needed.

Then the prosecution called its first witness. "Ashima Roy."

When Ashima was addressed directly, she stood. Her voice sounded steadier than it felt.

She replied precisely with what was required. Nothing more. Nothing less. The room did not tilt. The lights did not flicker. Nothing extraordinary occurred.

And yet, when she returned to her seat, she felt that something irrevocable had occurred. She no longer trusted the sequencing of her testimony. She had spoken accurately. She was no longer clear why. Ronnie moved close to her gently.

"Well done," he mumbled. She nodded. The move appeared automatic.

Victor observed her closely. Not her words. Her timing. He had seen that before in witnesses who had not lied but had surrendered sequences.

The case would not collapse today. But something important had shifted.

Isha's evidence was recorded that day, and on that premise alone, bail for Ronnie and Ashima was rejected.

That evening, Dr. Rosie sat alone in the improvised forensic office. She loosened her hair only after closing the door behind her. She secured it again before sitting down.

The autopsy papers lay open before her. She had reviewed it multiple times—every measurement, every notation, and every meticulously stated conclusion she herself had signed.

It was right. Defensible. Procedurally clean. And yet incomplete. Her eyes lingered on a single statement she had carefully softened days earlier: Cause of injuries consistent with blunt force trauma. Consistent but not exclusive. She grasped for her pen.

For a while, she debated modifying the statement. Clarifying the confusion, she had been permitted to remain.

A single clause would be enough to demand extra forensic research to buy Victor the time he had just been handed.

She realized how such a revision would be seen. She also recognized those it may protect or punish. Her hand lingered. This was not evidence manipulation. It was elucidation. Ethical. Justifiable.

And yet Dr. Rosie set the pen down. She closed the file instead.

If the truth necessitated intervention, it would have to surface without her bending it even slightly. The one concession she had assured herself she would never violate.

Still, as she shut off the light, she wondered quietly, unwillingly, whether Tolerance, too, may become a form of participation.

That night, Ashima lay awake, one hand resting instinctively on her tummy. She persuaded herself she had behaved for love. She persuaded herself that love was enough. But in the darkness, another concept snuck in silently and undesired. If Ronnie walked free tomorrow, he would never look back.

23 - The Benefit

The call came two days after the initial hearing. Not from the police. Not from the court. From someone whose viewpoint required no introduction.

The meeting was scheduled without haste and without secrecy, in an office near the courtroom—utilitarian, unremarkable, and chosen for its forgettability.

The man who greeted her spoke carefully, using the language of procedure rather than persuasion.

He complimented her for her cooperation so far. Not her testimony. Her consistency.

"There may be further attention," he said, almost shyly. "High-profile matters have a way of reopening themselves. We value continuity."

Naina understood what was expected. Not silence—she had already spoken. Stability.

He outlined the arrangement as if it were inconsequential. Short-term advisory work. Documentation review. Contextual support, if required. It would not interfere with proceedings. It would not require public association.

"You would not be asked to say anything new," he added.

"Only to remain available. And consistent."

The compensation was mentioned briefly, then set aside, as though money were the least relevant detail.

Naina asked a single question. "Is this connected to the case?"

The man smiled politely. "Everything nearby is," he said. "That doesn't make it improper."

She considered refusing—not out of principle, but reaction. Then she recognized the refusal for what it would be: performance. A gesture of distance where none existed.

She had already adjusted the clock. Already accepted the file's version of events over her memory. Saying no would not restore neutrality. It would only increase uncertainty.

She agreed. The man nodded once, pleased.

"This ensures there are no misunderstandings later," he said. "Situations like this benefit from continuity."

When she stepped back into the corridor, the courthouse seemed unchanged—voices echoing, papers moving, conclusions forming quietly behind closed doors. Nothing in the world had shifted. Only her position within it.

That night, in her hotel room, Naina replayed the conversation without emotion. There had been no threat. No pressure. Only an alignment that had made itself clear.

24 - The Advocate Who Looked Away

Saamiya Siddiqui recognized the problem before anyone called it. She recognized it in the transcript. Not the words—the space. Pauses that developed when none had been noted earlier. Answers that arrive a little late.

These corrections did not change anything but rather realigned the tone. She had been training long enough to spot the pattern.

Witnesses who lied left fingerprints. Witnesses who panicked released excess. Ashima Roy did neither. She drifted. Saamiya closed the file and rested back in her chair.

The chamber was quiet, isolated from the courtroom by thick walls and procedural privilege. This was where cases were actually shaped away from spectacle, closer to decision.

Ronnie sat across from her, hands folded neatly on the tabletop.

"She's fine," he said. "She testified exactly as we prepared."

Saamiya did not look at him. "She testified correctly," she said. "That's not the same thing."

Ronnie frowned slightly. "Meaning?"

"Meaning," Saamiya whispered, finally engaging his eyes,

"that she is no longer anchored to sequence." He said nothing.

Saamiya continued. "She didn't contradict herself. She didn't deviate. But she halted where she shouldn't have. She borrowed phrases unknowingly. She repaired time without realizing she was doing it."

Ronnie leaned forward. "Is that a problem?"

"It becomes one," Saamiya responded, "if someone chooses to press."

"Will they?"

Saamiya considered this. "No," she said.

"They won't," Ronnie whispered.

Relief went through him, fast and unexamined. Saamiya stuck out a finger. "Not because she's convincing," she continued. "But because she's inconvenient."

"Inconvenient how?"

"She complicates closure," Saamiya remarked.

"And closure is what everyone wants."

She opened another file, this one thinner.

"The prosecution will not pursue her aggressively," she continued. "They'll lean on material evidence. Forensics. Absence of weapon. Reasonable doubt. She will disappear from the center."

Ronnie nodded. This was okay.

"She won't be cross-examined again?" he asked.

"Until something forces it," Saamiya replied. "And nothing will."

He hesitated. "Is she... safe?"

Saamiya studied him carefully now.

"Legally?" she asked.

"Yes."

"Yes," she answered. "Because the court doesn't punish instability. It prevents it." She collected the files into a tidy stack, aligning their edges with exact taps.

"Your case," she said, "survives because you are consistent. You believe in control. That translates well."

Ronnie straightened unconsciously.

"Ashima," Saamiya went on, "believed in alignment. That's different. Alignment requires memory. Control only needs repetition."

Ronnie did not respond.

####

Later that day, Saamiya crossed paths with the prosecutor in the corridor. Their interaction was swift, courteous, and hollow.

"She's weakening," the prosecutor noted quietly.

"Yes," Saamiya said.

"You plan to re-examine her?"

"No," Saamiya said without hesitation.

"Neither do we," he replied.

They shared a stare of mutual understanding, not cooperation, but awareness.

Dragging Ashima back into evidence would break the narrative without aiding either side. It would raise questions no one wanted addressed. She was no longer helpful.

####

That evening, Ashima waited alone in the waiting area outside the courtroom. She had not been called again. No one informed her she wouldn't be.

She watched people pass—lawyers, clerks, and constables, each moving with purpose. She sought
to reconstruct where she was meant to travel next. The instruction did not arrive. She folded her hands. Unfolded them. Folded them again.

For the first time, the stillness around her was not interrogative. It was administrative. She was no longer a risk. She was no longer an asset. She had become something easy to manipulate. Invisible.

25 - What The Body Remembers

The body did not transform. That was the problem.

Dr. Rosie Panicker stood over the autopsy table with the same measured calm she had held since the night of December thirty-first.

The fluorescent lights above hummed quietly, impervious to interpretation.

The place smelled like antiseptic and metal—clean enough to look purposeful.

Riya Thapar lay precisely as she had before.

Rosie had studied the report twice earlier that morning. She acquired the language by heart.

Cause of death. Contributing factors. Absence of defensive wounds. Presence of toxins. Impact trauma connected with a blunt object.

Nothing had changed. Outside the room, however, everything had.

Court transcripts circulated. Timelines compressed. Statements acquired prominence. The case was becoming legible, a condition Rosie mistrusted much.

She lifted the file again. There it was, waiting. A term she could enhance. The blunt-force trauma was sufficient to cause death. She may add one

word. Primary.

Primary cause of death. It would not be a lie. The injuries supported it. The fracture pattern was clean. The power is decisive. The poison would remain documented, mentioned, and contextualized, but reduced.

Secondary. Incidental. That one adjustment would bolster the prosecution's case.

Rosie set the file down. She looked instead at the photographs strewn beside her. Close-ups of the wound.

The angle of impact. The absence of reluctance is striking. The body recalls force vividly. It did not editorialize. Bodies did not rearrange the sequence.

She removed her gloves and washed her hands longer than necessary, scraping at nothing. Water ran. Foam accumulated, then vanished.

When she returned, Victor was waiting just inside the doorway. He did not speak immediately. He rarely did.

"You're late," she commented.

"I was watching the testimony," he said.

She nodded once. "Then you saw it."

"Yes."

"Timing," she commented.

"Sequence," he corrected.

Rosie grabbed up the file again, tapping it carefully against the table to align the pages.

"She didn't lie," Victor observed.

"No," Rosie agreed. "She misplaced it."

"That's worse," he said.

Rosie did not argue. She flipped to the toxicology report.

"Poison impaired her," she claimed.

"Slowed reaction. Reduced coordination. It did not kill her."

Victor leaned closer. "And the blow?"

"Conclusive," Rosie said.

"But overlapping." She paused.

"Which gives the defense room,"

Victor added. "Yes."

She could still rectify that. She may restrict the room.

Rosie reached for her pen. The nib hovered over the paper. She imagined the courtroom again. The judge is nodding. The defense is recalibrating. The case is clean, procedural, and reasonable. She imagined Ashima on the stand, arguing not with truth but with order. The pen did not move. Instead, Rosie emphasized a different section.

Time of injury cannot be assigned to a single incident with complete precision. She pressed harder than needed, making a faint impression on the paper below.

Victor observed her closely. "You're leaving it unstable," he said.

"I'm leaving it honest," Rosie responded.

He considered that. "Honesty collapses cases," he noted.

"Sometimes," she said. "It also exposes them." She closed the file.

In the calm that followed, Rosie was conscious of a mild pressure in her chest—not concern, but consequence. By refusing to prefer one mechanism above another, she had continued uncertainty. Ambiguity would not secure Ashima. It would secure the record. Victor said again, gentler now.

"If it fails, it won't be because of lack of evidence."

Rosie met his eyes. "No. It will be because people confuse coherence with truth." He nodded once.

She turned back to the corpse. Riya Thapar did not look serene. She appeared finished. Rosie knew bodies did not care what survived. They remembered what transpired. And they waited.

26 - Interrogation As Climate

Ronnie stood alone in the restroom, clutching the porcelain edge of the sink as if it were the only thing anchoring him to the room.

He wore a simple shirt and plain trousers, creased from hours of sitting, damp at the collar where sweat had gathered without his noticing.

He splashed water on his face, watching it bead on skin he no longer recognized. His hairline had begun to recede unevenly—something he had avoided noticing until now. The image in the mirror seemed older than the night had made him: creased, withered, and unfamiliar.

He tried to recall the last time he had loved Riya. Nothing came. Prison did not terrify him. Irrelevance did. To be reduced to a footnote felt, to him, like a new form of erasure. Even now—especially now—she was the only reason his name still mattered.

The interrogation room was a controlled atmosphere of pressure. Three spaces fused into one purpose: the austere interrogation room itself, a dim observation chamber behind a one-way mirror, and the narrow hallway outside, where footfalls echoed like judgment.

Ronnie sat at the metal table as questioning began, his shirt clinging weakly to his back, the fabric no longer crisp enough to communicate authority or dominance. The chair was too low. His knees pressed painfully against the table, forcing him to lean forward.

Present were Victor, Inspector Daulat Talpade, and Dr. Rosie.

Across from Ronnie sat his lawyer, Saamiya Siddiqui—cautious, watchful, and prepared to defend him from himself if necessary. Her pen lay exactly parallel to the table's edge, undisturbed since she had sat down.

There was a shift in the room. Victor was no longer merely tolerated; he was approved. The court had granted him broad powers of inquiry, and everyone knew it.

Victor stood near the table, inspecting the photographs arranged with deliberate order. He studied them longer than necessary—not because he failed to understand them, but because he understood how they would be perceived.

"These injuries," Dr. Rosie said, displaying the images, "suggest persistence."

Victor nodded once. He briefly shaded his eyes from the glare, then let his hand fall. There was no way to soften what daylight insisted upon.

"Eventually," he said. "But we don't need to frame that yet."

Rosie looked at him—suddenly, precisely. Not confrontationally.

"Yet?" she asked.

Victor adjusted the file, aligning the pages. Order mattered, especially early.

"Some conclusions survive better," he said, "when they arrive later."

Rosie made a note. Her pen paused—not at the content of the revelation, but at his assertion. Timing as doctrine. Delay as a method.

Victor observed the quiet and chose not to acknowledge it. Delay, he told himself, was not distortion. Timing was strategy. Strategy was the difference between truth uncovered and truth rejected. He had always believed this. He still did.

He broke the stillness. "Ronnie, where is the vase?"

Saamiya answered immediately, without looking at him. "My client is not required to answer that question."

She did not look at Ronnie as she spoke. Her gaze remained fixed ahead, as if bodies were distractions.

Victor nodded. "Very well. Let's change the question."

Ronnie looked up.

"Have you been experiencing hair loss recently?"

Ronnie frowned. "What kind of question is that?"

Saamiya's tone sharpened. "Mr. Victor, confine yourself to matters relevant to the case."

"This question is relevant," Victor replied.

A pause.

"Yes," Ronnie said, uncertain. "I've been losing hair."

"Good," Victor said.

"Then perhaps you can explain how your hair samples were found by the forensic team in Ashima Roy's bed, her washroom, and her shower area. In fact, on nearly every surface of her private quarters."

Saamiya leaned toward Ronnie.

"Do not answer," Victor continued, unperturbed. "No matter how strongly you advise silence, the evidence already speaks. And what it says is this: Mr. Grewal was a frequent visitor to Ms. Roy's room."

"An affair, perhaps?"

Ronnie sneered weakly. "Oh, come on. Maybe I went there for business."

Victor tilted his head.

"Business?" His voice tightened. "Ronnie, you were removed from all of Riya Thapar's enterprises a year ago. Your projects had already collapsed. So tell me—what business compelled you to enter your wife's secretary's bedroom?"

Ronnie hesitated. "Maybe... to use the bathroom."

Victor almost smiled. "There are nine washrooms in that villa. Yet you consistently chose hers."

He leaned forward. "Why not admit that something inappropriate was happening between you and Ashima?"

Saamiya cut in sharply. "These are speculative allegations. My client will not respond."

Victor inhaled slowly. "Ms. Siddiqui, everything appears baseless to you. This case. The murder. The law."

He slid several photographs across the table. "Please look at these."

The images lay exposed between them, unambiguous.

"In these photographs," Victor continued, "Ronnie Grewal and Ashima Roy are seen in a compromised position."

His voice softened deliberately. "I did not wish to present these. Ashima appears in them as well. She is a woman."

He hesitated, then spoke gently. "And dignity—especially a woman's dignity—has consequences. That is why I have chosen not to present this material in court yet. I do not wish to make it public at this time."

Dr. Rosie shifted slightly in her chair. Her sleeves were rolled just enough to free her wrists—no more.

For a moment—only a moment—her hand moved toward the photographs. Not to examine them, but to turn them face down. The impulse startled her. She stopped herself, fingertips brushing the smooth surface before returning to her lap.

Her expression remained neutral. But something had tightened beneath it. She knew what Victor was doing. She also understood why it worked.

Saamiya held Victor's gaze. She said nothing. The silence stretched long enough to make it clear that she understood—and rejected—the implication.

"Ashima is seated in the adjacent room," Victor said. "Imagine what happens when these photographs are shown to her." He closed the file halfway.

"She is not as shameless as you seem to think—hiding behind procedure while her life collapses."

Saamiya stiffened. For the first time, her fingers curled around the pen, thumb pressing into the metal clip before releasing it. Victor noticed.

"There's something else you should know," he said.

Saamiya's pen halted mid-motion.

"Ashima is pregnant."

The room changed. No one moved. No one spoke. Ronnie's face emptied, the muscles in his jaw tightening as if bracing against impact.

Victor continued, his tone unchanged. "She refuses abortion. She believes she loves you."

A pause.

"You, however, do not want the child."

Somewhere within the building, a clock chimed softly. Mechanical. Indifferent.

"If this pregnancy becomes public," Victor said, "both of you—Ronnie and Ashima—will go inside for a long time."

He turned fully to Saamiya. "Tell me, Ms. Siddiqui," he said quietly, "is the child growing inside Ashima also baseless?"

No one answered.

"This truth will surface," Victor continued. "Today or tomorrow."

He gathered the files. "So whatever you need to do—or say—start preparing now. It would be wiser."

The room stayed silent.

Saamiya collected her papers with meticulous care, restoring the pen to its exact position before standing, as if order itself were worth preserving.

Dr. Rosie remained seated a minute longer than permitted.

She had nearly intervened. She had chosen not to.

And she knew that choice would not feel neutral again.

27 - The Client Who Couldn't Be Saved

Long before Ronnie would sit across from her in custody, Saamiya Siddiqui had believed in absolutes.

In her early years at the bar, she had been difficult to ignore. She argued with precision and refused shortcuts, speaking clearly in rooms where women were expected to listen and wait their turn. Men mistook her calm for arrogance and her persistence for provocation. She believed fully, almost naively, that law was sufficient armor, that clarity and correctness would always prevail if pressed firmly enough.

That belief lasted until one case.

The opposition belonged to a family whose influence did not require legality. When argument failed, warnings arrived—delivered publicly enough to be unmistakable, privately enough to leave no record. Outside the court, she learned what persistence cost women who did not know when to stop.

No complaint was registered. No protection was offered.

The message worked without being enacted. The case collapsed soon after, not on merit, but on caution.

Saamiya did not leave the profession. She left absolutes.

She learned to negotiate outcomes rather than demand them. To read rooms before speaking. To protect clients by limiting exposure instead of escalating conflict. Justice, she learned, was not abandoned all at once. It was adjusted incrementally according to what the system was willing to defend.

Years later, that recalibration sat quietly beneath everything she did. Including Ronnie.

He had once been careful. Disciplined. A man whose charm was engineered rather than impulsive. Saamiya had known him personally, intimately, within boundaries that had been explicitly agreed upon. Even after her marriage, the relationship had remained contained, consensual, controlled, and deliberate. She had trusted him not because he was harmless, but because he was precise. She knew now that she had not been immune to him.

When Ronnie and Ashima came to her as clients, something already felt wrong. The file was thin. The opposition was heavy with implication. Every assurance she offered sounded rehearsed, even to herself. She knew, before anyone said it aloud, that the case would not survive long.

Victor's findings reached her quietly, not formally, not in writing, but clearly enough. Clearly enough to separate charm from deceit. Clearly enough to recognize that Ronnie and Ashima was not a client in trouble but a pattern nearing collapse.

By the time Constable Gopinath Patil unlocked the door and propelled Ronnie inside, Saamiya already knew the truth.

The lock clicked before the door opened.

Ronnie entered custody stripped of presentation. He wore a plain shirt and trousers, creased and damp at the collar, the kind of clothes slept in rather than chosen. Whatever performance he usually carried had been confiscated. His body leaned forward as though confrontation followed him by habit, bristling, impatient, and offended by containment.

The moment he saw her, he erupted.

"What are you even doing?" he shouted. "How long do you expect me to stay here? Do you have any idea who I am? This is all nonsense, absolute rubbish!"

The words poured out, complaints stacking on accusations, entitlement disguised as outrage. His voice ricocheted around the room, angry, pleading, indignant, and looping back on itself.

Saamiya did not interrupt.

She stood a few steps away, dressed in a finely tailored suit—the kind worn by advocates when they were not appearing before judges but negotiating beyond them. Her hair was pulled back neatly. She looked finished. Complete.

She watched him calmly and thought, with a clarity that surprised even her: What a deeply dishonest man.

She raised one finger. Not sharply. Not theatrically. She pointed to the chair opposite her.

"Sit," she said.

The word cut through him.

Ronnie stopped mid-sentence, stared at her, then dropped into the chair. His breath was uneven, restless energy still vibrating in his limbs. The authority in the room shifted without announcement.

She sat across from him, crossing her legs quietly. The dilemma before her was not legal. It was moral. Lawyers defended. Doctors healed. Neither should excuse deliberate harm by pretending not to see it. Truth was the only currency that mattered.

"No one can save you now," Saamiya said gently. "Not even me."

Ronnie blinked.

"I only came to tell you that," she added.

For a second, he looked startled. Then he laughed, a brittle, overstretched sound.

"Come on, Saamiya," he said quickly. "Don't overreact. I'm sorry I was angry. I took it out on you. I'm under pressure. Try to understand."

Apologies braided themselves into excuses. Stress was blamed for violence. Circumstances are blamed for choices.

Saamiya listened and felt something settle.

This is where he belongs, she thought. Contained. Limited. Unable to improvise harm.

"You were always such a big player," she said quietly. "Your charm worked differently. Women trusted you."

Ronnie smiled instinctively. Saamiya did not.

"I wasn't immune," she continued. "I fell for it too."

His smile faded.

"But it was an open relationship," she said. "Even after my marriage, we stayed within boundaries. With consent. With control."

She leaned forward slightly.

"So why," she asked evenly, "did you get Ashima pregnant?"

Ronnie stiffened.

"You always played safe," she went on. "So what happened? Couldn't stop yourself? Or is the old Ronnie already dead?"

The question landed heavier than an accusation.

She paused, then said coldly, “I have never lost a case in my life. I will lose this one only because of you.”

Ronnie opened his mouth. Closed it.

“I warned you,” she said, standing and smoothing the edge of her jacket. “Never mix business with personal appetite.”

She looked down at him—really looked.

“Pray,” she said at last, “that Himmat Singh and that vase are never found.”

She turned toward the door.

“Saamiyawait,” Ronnie cried, panic finally unmasking him. “You can’t leave me like this.”

She stopped at the threshold. Did not turn around.

“I already have,” she said.

The door closed.

Ronnie remained seated, clothes rumpled, voice drained, charm extinguished, alone with the first reality he could no longer argue away.

Earlier, the client had sat across from her, hopeful, the way people were when the procedure still resembled protection. Saamiya had said, We’ll do what we can.

It hadn’t been a lie. It had been a recalibration. And this time, even that would not be enough.

28 - Daylight Was Unforgiving

Dr. Rosie continued through the material with professional restraint, her words concise and precise.

Victor listened with his fists clenched behind his back, nodding where appropriate. He had mastered the appearance of attention. What he had not mastered was the silence inside his own head.

They returned to Riya's villa, the accident site, and the neighboring roads in daylight.

Dust settled openly on every surface now. Nothing veiled beneath darkness. Night forgave too much. Daylight provided no mercy.

At the roadside, Dr. Rosie stopped unexpectedly and squatted, scrutinizing the surface. Victor stood a few steps behind her.

Distance had become instinctive; he found himself moving back without remembering taking the step.

"These tire impressions are inconsistent," she commented. "They indicate more than one visit." Victor waited.

Silence usually indicated more than inquiry.

"Same vehicle," she continued. "Overlapping tracks.

Identical alignment."

She stood and faced him. Victor nodded once. Outwardly composed. Inwardly, something transformed. Twice.

His attention drifted to the unfinished papers on his desk. The meeting was postponed until after the holidays. Delay, he had told himself, was caution, not recklessness. Procedure. Prudence. Reasonable restraint.

Inside the villa, sunlight slashed across the living room at sharp angles, exposing dust undisturbed since the night Riya died.

Dr. Rosie put up the postmortem photographs with painstaking care. She aligned the photographs neatly, edges squared to the table, as if mathematics might compel order where a tale could not.

"The head injuries were not accidental," she claimed. "This was a sustained assault." She indicated precise spots.

"Multiple impacts. Same weapon. Force employed after incapacitation."

Victor studied the photographs longer than necessary.

"This was not a lack of control," she stressed. "It was persistence."

Dr. Rosie grasped for the next photograph and hesitated. Her fingers lingered over the print. For a brief second, she gazed not at Victor but at the light across the table, recalibrating something inside.

"There is," she said slowly, "one inference that could be drawn." Victor paused.

"If the sequence of blows were framed differently," she continued, "it could suggest an initial accidental impact followed by panic. Not intent. Not persistence." She inhaled, measured.

"That interpretation would not survive rigorous scrutiny," she added. "But it would survive headlines." Her hand lowered, not onto the image, but flat on the table.

"I considered noting it," she said. "Briefly. As a conceivable possibility."

She met Victor's glance. "I chose not to." The stillness that followed was heavier than before.

"Why?" Victor asked, though he suspected the answer.

"Because once it exists on paper," Dr. Rosie said, "others can weaponize it. And this case already has enough weapons."

She placed the photo back into the file and closed it with quiet resolve.

"I am here to interpret evidence," she answered. "Not to provide escape routes for rehearsed narratives."

Victor moved back, noticing a faint reflection of himself in the glass cabinet. For a moment, he wondered whether Riya had seen the same hesitancy in him that he now disliked in others.

Dr. Rosie also highlighted in her report that fentanyl was identified in Riya's circulation, with traces around her nostrils.

There was a possibility of overdose that would worsen physiological stress and could precipitate heart collapse.

After a pause, Victor remarked. "There are two trials underway," he remarked. "One in court. One in public."

Dr. Rosie closed the file. "In the media," Victor added, "Saamiya Siddiqui has already concluded the case. Robbery Murder Clean. Convenient."

He hesitated. "I didn't challenge it early enough."

The admission happened too late to impact anything beyond his knowledge of it.

"Cases used to be fought on competence," he continued quietly. "Now they're fought on presentation."

Victor had once thought truth could protect itself. He loosened his collar, then tightened it again. The motion brought no relief. Experience had fixed him.

Truth needed intervention, and sometimes he had been delayed. Dr. Rosie straightened.

"From a legal standpoint," she said, "Ronnie has forfeited all financial claims. Insurance funds and estate administration have passed to Desai & Associates, in keeping with the decedent's final directives." She hesitated. "He is insolvent."

Victor gazed toward the window, sunshine shining furiously off the glass.

"And Ashima?" he asked.

"If her involvement was transactional," Dr. Rosie remarked, "then she miscalculated. Continued participation with Ronnie has ensured her downfall."

"How are you aware of Ashima's pregnancy?" Dr. Rosie asked.

"For the past month," Victor began, "I was observing them at Riya's request." He paused. "She trusted me to act if things escalated." The words stayed between them.

"We were supposed to meet on the first of January," he stated. "I had everything: financial trails, communications, leverage. Inspector Ghosh was assisting. On the night of the thirty-first, after hours, we were pondering future steps."

His voice fell. "That's when the wireless message came in: Riya Thapar Homicide."

Each repetition added increasing weight.

"All the evidence I had became procedurally irrelevant." He

stared down at his hands. "But before she died," he said, "she did one decisive thing."

Victor touched the inside pocket of his coat. "She officially emailed me and appointed me as her legal representative." A pause. "She acted when I didn't."

He met Dr. Rosie's eyes.

"Without that email," he said, "I would have remained precisely what I was: aware, knowledgeable, and inactive."

The calm that followed carried no reproach. Only recognition.

Later that evening, back in Victor's room, neither of them spoke about work.

The silence was not awkward; it was weighted. They opened a bottle without ceremony, the soft pop of the cork sounding louder than it should have. One drink became another—not from intention, but from exhaustion, from the quiet relief of not having to explain themselves to anyone.

They sat close without noticing when the space between them diminished. Conversation drifted—from examples to memories, from professional constraint to things postponed so long they had lost their names. Laughter came unexpectedly, then faded into something more careful. The closeness was not planned. It arrived the way sleep does—gradually, and then all at once.

Rosie knew she could stop it. That she should.

The knowledge hovered, present but unattended.

Victor never pushed. He never had to. There was an ease in the way he moved, in how he listened—his attention steady, unclaimed, yet absolute. When his hand brushed hers, it did not linger. That restraint was what undid her. His passion had never been about urgency. It had always been about inevitability.

She felt herself yielding not to him, but to something she had lived without for eight years.

Affection without calculation. Touch without consequence.

When he finally reached for her, it was with familiarity tempered by time—careful, almost reverent. As if he were relearning her and allowing himself to be relearned in return.

The world narrowed to warmth and breath, to the remembered the language of bodies that had once known each other intimately and still did, despite everything.

That night, Rosie felt protected. Comforted. As though the world had, briefly, lowered its defenses.

She noticed the change in him—the intensity sharpened by years of restraint rather than dulled by absence. There was a quiet power beneath his control now. Not aggression.

Endurance. A persistence that came from surviving loss and still choosing to feel. It was the same stubbornness he brought to his work—a refusal to let what mattered slip into abstraction. Something real had been claimed, and once claimed, it demanded acknowledgment.

In the freezing hours before dawn, Rosie lay awake, her body still holding warmth where it should not have remained. Memory lingered in sensation. In the way his presence had steadied her breathing. In how easy it had felt to belong again.

Morning light offered perspective. Dr. Rosie awakened first. The realization came swiftly, decisively. Whatever comfort the night had offered, it had crossed a boundary neither of them could pretend was temporary. They had divorced for reasons that had not dissolved with time or touch.

By the time Victor woke, she was already dressed.

"This shouldn't have happened," she said gently—not accusatory, but certain.

He nodded. He did not try to stop her.

They parted without drama, reassembling the professional distance they both understood was necessary. Some faults are not loud. They do not announce themselves when they are made. They are quiet. And irreversible.

29 - The Only Way That Remained

By the time Saamiya arrived, the court parking lot was already full.

Cars crept between painted lines, drivers scanning for space with the tired patience of people who had learned not to expect convenience.

Exhaust hung low in the heat. Nothing moved quickly unless forced to.

Inspector Daulat stood beside his car, jacket unzipped against the morning warmth. He had the posture of someone waiting without admitting to it—still, unhurried, as if time were something that obeyed him.

Saamiya parked two rows away and left the engine running. Through the windshield, she studied him: the ease in his stance, the lack of urgency, and the way he occupied the space without claiming it.

Then she turned off the ignition and stepped out.

"Leaving the case?" Daulat asked as she approached.

She didn't slow down.

"I'm done stabilizing something that shouldn't survive."

He nodded, as though confirming a diagnosis. "That's unfortunate."

"It's necessary," she said.

They stopped between their cars, dust and smog thickening the air around them.

"This doesn't go to trial cleanly," Saamiya continued. "You know that."

"Trials don't require clean," Daulat replied. "They require coherence."

She looked at him then. "And this has neither."

"It can," he said. "If we stop pretending everyone needs to be saved."

Saamiya crossed her arms. "Ronnie isn't salvageable without collapsing everything else."

Daulat stepped closer—not invasive, not familiar. Just enough to make the distance instructional.

"There is one way," he said.

She waited.

"A single testimony," he continued. "Responsibility redirected. One figure made central."

Saamiya exhaled. "You mean Ashima."

"Yes."

"And Ronnie?"

"Repositioned," Daulat said calmly. "As cooperative. As a witness."

The word settled between them. Cars passed behind them. Doors opened. Voices rose and fell. No one noticed the conversation.

"You want me to sign off on sacrificing her," Saamiya said.

Daulat corrected her gently. "I want you to preserve what can still be preserved."

She shook her head. "That isn't preservation. It's an exchange."

"Everything is," he said.

Her gaze drifted toward the courthouse entrance. People were already queuing at security, files tucked under their arms, disputes rehearsed and ready.

"And Naina?" she asked.

Something in Daulat's expression shifted—not concern, but calculation.

"She can be managed," he said. "She's already proven cooperative."

Saamiya closed her eyes briefly.

"You'll speak to Ronnie," she said at last. "Not me."

Daulat inclined his head. "Of course."

"And if Naina refuses?"

"Then we adjust."

Saamiya gathered her folders.

"One condition," she said.

He waited.

"This doesn't come back to me. I don't deliver the offer."

Daulat smiled faintly. "You're still leaving the case?"

She hesitated.

"I'm still telling myself I am."

By then, the parking lot had already erased the conversation. Cars moved. People passed. Nothing remained of it but the decision.

30 - What Can Be Bought, And What Cannot

Naina did not reach for the folder. She glanced at it, then back at them: Daulat near the window, Saamiya with her hands folded, and Ronnie leaning forward as if proximity might still matter.

"This is a large reward," she said.

Ronnie nodded. "It reflects the importance of your role."

"It reflects the importance of silence," she replied.

"Just not mine."

Daulat spoke evenly. "You've already accepted compensation once."

"Yes," Naina said. "And I delivered exactly what I was paid for."

Saamiya leaned forward slightly. "That was cooperation."

"And this," Naina said, "is authorship."

The word held.

"If I testify against Ashima," she continued, "there will be no ambiguity left. No room for repositioning. You won't need me again."

"That's the point," Ronnie said.

"That's the danger," Naina replied.

She stepped to the table not to take the folder, but to close it herself. Her fingertips rested on the cover, deliberate.

"This money doesn't buy my voice," she said. "It buys my disappearance."

No one objected. Daulat watched her.

"You're refusing a significant reward."

"I'm refusing finality."

Saamiya's expression shifted—not relief, not guilt. Recognition.

Ronnie spoke again, quieter. "You're making this harder than it needs to be."

Naina turned toward the door. "No," she said. "I'm making it visible."

She paused with her hand on the knob.

"For the record," she added, without looking back, "I will not testify against Ashima."

The statement wasn't defiant. It was administrative.

The door closed softly behind her. Inside, nothing moved.

Daulat spoke first. "She understands the system."

Saamiya nodded. "Which is why she won't save it."

Ronnie remained seated, staring at the unopened folder.

The case, though nominally complete, had begun to resist alignment.

31 - The Tiffin Box

The tiffin box arrived shortly after noon.

It was set on the corner of Ashima's desk without announcement—stainless steel, clean, normal.

The lid had been fixed neatly, the way they secured things when they didn't want attention.

Ashima glanced at it longer than needed.

Meals have been inconsistent since the arrest. Sometimes forgotten. Sometimes denied. Habit mattered more than hunger.

She opened the parcel. Rice. Lentils. Vegetables placed tastefully. Nothing fancy. Nothing is wrong.

She lifted the second container and paused. A folded slip of paper sat underneath it, pressed flat on the metal. Ashima did not touch it immediately.

Notes have become dangerous things. They suggested purpose. They welcomed blame. She had learned to live without them.

Carefully, she unfolded it. There were no names. No details. No instructions.

Only two lines.

Ronnie is to testify as a corroborating witness.

Ashima is positioned as the main planner.

Responsibility consolidated. An external witness must be sought. Ashima read it once. Then she folded it and placed it into her pocket. There was nothing to comprehend. Nothing to disagree with. The message did not ask her to edit anything. It validated what she had already determined. She closed the tiffin box. The dinner remained untouched.

When the police called her in again, she rose slowly. Too slowly. She took two steps toward the doorway. Then she staggered.

Someone reached for her arm. She let her weight go before they could steady her. Her knees folded gently. Her head leaned forward. She smacked the floor hard enough to be credible. Voices rose. Chairs scraped back.

An appeal went out for medical help. Ashima kept her eyes closed. Her breathing was shallow. Irregular. Perfect.

By the time they raised her, the chamber had already adjusted its position. Concern replaced suspicion. Urgency replaced questioning.

As she was taken out, she felt it strongly. This was not a collapse. That was timing. Payback, she discovered, did not always come standing. It came horizontally at times.

32 - The Body That Refused

Silence and light came before awareness.

Ashima opened her eyes to the sound of a monitor tracking time she had not agreed to surrender. A nurse stood nearby, confirming data. Outside a curtain, a doctor murmured, "Stress response, dehydration—we'll confirm."

Ashima wanted to move. Her body answered slowly, as if permission were being negotiated.

The doctor noticed her eyes open and stepped closer. "You fainted," he said. "Your blood pressure dropped."

She stared at the ceiling.

"There's something else," he added. "A routine test."

The confirmation arrived without drama. Pregnant.

The word was delivered neutrally, as if it belonged to a chart rather than a life.

Ashima closed her eyes. Fear came first—pure, immediate, physical. Fear of exposure. Of vulnerability. Of being observed without armor. Then anger returned, sharper now. Focused.

By twilight, the hospital corridor had grown congested. Voices moved differently. Phones rang too often. A television near the nurses' station repeated a headline:

PRIME MURDER ACCUSED PREGNANT: INVESTIGATION COMPLICATES

Ashima watched its reflection in the chrome stand. So this, she thought, is what cannot be changed. Tears came again, but they did not weaken her. They released, not collapsed. Her shoulders shook once, then steadied. They had hoped to use stillness against her to translate discipline into disappearance.

Instead, her body had intervened. Not as defense. As an interruption. Her weakness, long hidden and endured, was now public. Documented. Time-stamped. Broadcast. It could not be cross-examined. It could not be withdrawn. It could not lie.

She opened her eyes. Somewhere beyond the hospital gates, plans were being revised. Testimonies recalculated. Offers are losing value by the hour.

Ronnie would grasp it quickly. Daulat already had. Whoever authored the statement would understand most of all. Ashima did not smile. She did not feel victorious. She felt still. For the first time since the night of the murder, the system was reacting to something it could not manage. And it was growing inside her.

33 - A Room That Refused Air

Victor walked toward Isha's quarters as the wind gathered strength.

The air carried the faint scent of soap and damp cloth—laundry done recently, carefully. It moved low along the ground, slipping between buildings, lifting dust and the darker smell of wet soil from the trees surrounding Riya's villa. The wind felt deliberate, as though it were searching for seams.

The quarters stood slightly apart from the rest of the property, half concealed, pressed against the edge of the land like something that preferred not to be acknowledged. Inside, the air was still. Too still. The stillness did not receive him; it closed around him, compressing, windowless, watchful.

Isha sat across from him without moving. Her sleeves were drawn down despite the heat, her hands hidden from view. Her posture was controlled, almost reduced, as though she had folded herself inward long before he arrived. Nothing about her suggested openness—not resistance, not fear. Containment.

Outside, the wind struck a loose shutter, rattling it sharply before the sound was swallowed by the walls.

"I'm going to ask directly," Victor said. "Why are you so certain Ronnie and Ashima are responsible?"

Her eyes did not move.

His voice carried the neutral cadence of investigation, language shaped by method rather than accusation.

"Duty?" he asked. "Or something else?"

Silence.

Yet beneath the structure of his questions, another meaning pressed closer.

Victor went on, carefully. "Ronnie Grewal has a reputation. He doesn't respect limits. He confuses access with permission."

The wind rattled a shutter outside, sharp and brief.

"He enters spaces he doesn't belong in," Victor added. "He takes what he assumes is available."

Isha's jaw tightened. Just once.

"Did he ever cross a line?" Victor asked. "With you?"

She stared past him.

"Is this revenge?" he asked quietly.

Outside, the wind surged again, striking the walls with sudden force before retreating. Isha did not flinch.

Only her jaw tightened once, then relaxed. Her gaze stayed fixed, distant, as though her attention were anchored somewhere far beyond the room.

When she spoke, her voice was flat, formal, and almost rehearsed.

"I have already given my statement to the police," she said. "I have testified in court. I have nothing further to say."

There was no hesitation. No defensiveness. No attempt at clarification. The words landed evenly, closing the exchange. The silence that followed felt deliberately constructed, forming a confinement more absolute than any locked door.

Victor's attention drifted to a framed photograph on the wall. It was old. A red Fiat, open-roofed. A child seated on Himmat Singh's lap, three small girls pressed close beside him. The image carried a density the room itself seemed to avoid acknowledging.

She looked at him then. Briefly.

"It's late," Isha said. "You should leave."

He understood then that she was not concealing the truth. She was guarding it.

When Victor stepped outside, the air struck his face sharply, as if the night itself were attempting to rouse him. He lifted his collar against the chill, then let it fall open again. The cold felt different now—more insistent.

He looked back once at the quarters. From the outside, they appeared small. Contained. But he sensed something vast and unsettled held within them, something that resisted exposure by refusing to expand.

Sleep would not come that night. The ceiling above his bed felt too close, the darkness pressing inward. His thoughts traced the same absences again and again—missing pieces, statements that were truthful but incomplete, silences that carried more weight than confession.

The problem no longer felt like something to be solved. It felt like a sealed, airless chamber, waiting for him to uncover what had been trapped inside all along.

Part V

Revelation

34 - The Second Visit

Detective Victor met Naina at Hotel Hilltop's restaurant patio. The midnight air was cool, dense with the aroma of damp pine.

The night of the thirty-first hung between them, unresolved and persistent.

Naina wore the same restricted palette she had worn throughout: black, grey, and nothing reflective. Her hair fell naturally, unstyled, depriving her of attention.

Victor appeared uncomfortable. He explained he had solved several cases, but Riya worried him. The haste with which the offenders had found it appeared indecent.

Something had been odd from the outset. And yet, without the murder weapon, the case had gone beyond his grasp.

Dr. Rosie had been disappointed. Inspector Daulat Talpade has shown himself to be corrupt beyond doubt. Saamiya Siddiqui has used her influence to hinder the prosecution. Everything had aligned and meant nothing.

"And Himmat Singh," Victor continued, almost to himself. "He's still not been found."

He shook his head slightly. "If he had been," he said, "things might have been very different." "Let's have coffee."

The diner was a café with self-service. Victor brought coffee for Naina. He placed the cup gently, sleeves brushing the table edge.

His hands stayed there a little longer than needed. His outfit smelled strongly of travel and paper.

"Your favorite," he said. "Black coffee, with less sugar."

Naina glanced up. "You seem to know a lot about my tastes and preferences."

"That's my job, actually," Victor said. "Finding people's secrets, understanding them."

"In the previous few days, you've already dug quite extensively into everyone's lives." She glanced toward the darkening hills. "This is Palankhet, sir. Many mysteries are concealed here. Don't dig them up."

"That's my responsibility too," Victor responded quietly. "Knowing everyone's secrets." There was a pause.

"Professionally," Naina added, "your work may be to uncover secrets. But don't go so deep that you become a mystery yourself."

She did not look at him as she said it. "This city," she commented, "has swallowed many people."

Victor could not respond fast.

"It shouldn't happen," Naina went on, "that you go to sleep one night and never wake up. That this becomes your last evening."

"So it's preferable if certain secrets stay buried." Victor remarked calmly, "For instance, someone's second visit to Riya's villa on the night of the 31st. Dr. Rosie has already recognized the double tire marks from that car."

She grinned faintly. Not an agreement. Recognition.

Victor raised his hands slightly. "Don't worry, ma'am. This isn't an official interrogation."

He turned his palms outward. "Look, I'm not recording anything. I'm not writing anything. I merely want to comprehend what actually happened."

Naina studied him now longer than before. "Well, Mr. Victor," she replied at last, "you are remarkable. No one can outthink you."

She paused, then added, almost conversationally, "You detected double markings from someone's car. But a strong individual like Himmat Singh can't be found."

She finally glanced at him. "That's quite something."

Victor retained her gaze. There was no defensiveness in him now, only tiredness. He stood. He nodded once in assent without conclusion.

"Sometimes," she observed, "it's better if unresolved parts of a story are left untouched. Otherwise, the tale never reaches its lovely ending."

As he went away, he grasped something fully for the first time.

35 - What Was Slipped Under The Door

Victor reached his hotel room close to midnight.

The corridor was deserted. The carpet muted his steps, the way hotels were designed to soften everything—movement, memory, consequence. He unlocked the door and stepped inside. The light was off.

As his hand moved toward the switch, he saw it.

A folded sheet of paper lay just inside the room, placed with care. It had been slid beneath the door and creased once, precisely, so it would not tear.

Victor did not pick it up at once.

He looked down the hallway. Empty. No voices. No footsteps. No movement. He closed the door, locked it, then bent and retrieved the paper.

There was no handwriting he recognized. No letterhead. No mark of origin. Only a sentence.

Behind the third teak tree, beyond the eastern boundary wall, buried beneath exposed roots.

Nothing else. No signature. No threat. No explanation.

Victor sat on the edge of the bed and read it again. The specificity unsettled him. This was not speculation. Not a suggestion. This was instruction.

He examined the paper for impressions, for residue, for anything traceable. There was nothing. Whoever had written it did not want recognition. They wanted the result.

The implication came quickly. If the object was found, the case would close—not because truth had surfaced, but because the system would finally possess something it could file. Ronnie and Ashima would be convicted. The sender understood this.

Victor folded the paper once and slipped it into his pocket. He did not photograph it. He did not log it. He did not report it.

By morning, it would either be real or it would vanish. Either way, it would leave no record.

He did not sleep.

Instead, he went to Dr. Rosie.

He told her everything. Not selectively. Not strategically. He placed the paper between them and let it sit there, a third presence at the table.

"I couldn't keep that from you," he said. "Not after everything."

Rosie read the message once. Then again. Her expression did not change.

"This is a shortcut," she said at last.

"Yes," Victor replied. "And it works."

"That's what worries me."

A familiar stillness settled between them—dense, weighted by everything they had stopped pretending not to see.

Victor looked at her. Not at the paper. Not at the files. At her.

The same unspoken impulse surfaced—clear, unambiguous. The desire to stay. To recreate the brief, fragile interval when the edges of everything had softened. Rosie felt it too. For a moment, it flickered between them—quiet, dangerous.

Then she closed the file.

"By morning," she said, "I have to submit the forensic report in court."

Her voice was calm. Unemotional.

"My workload has doubled. Every line will be examined. Every word will matter."

Personal feeling was set aside—not abruptly, not cruelly, but with discipline. Like instruments returned to their case after use.

Victor nodded. He understood what limitation looked like when it was chosen rather than imposed.

Rosie stood, gathering her papers. “This can’t happen again,” she said—not unkindly, but without room for discussion.

Victor did not respond.

After she left, he remained seated for a long time. Then he exhaled slowly, quietly. Not in frustration.

In acknowledgment.

Some nights delivered answers. Others only clarified the cost of knowing them.

36 - Confession That Shook The Night

That night, the news breaks without warning.

It spreads across television screens in bursts of light and sound, interrupting scheduled programming, seizing attention before anyone can prepare for it.

Himmat Singh appears live, escorted and framed by the media.

He sits slightly bowed, wrapped in a coarse woolen shawl despite the mild weather. It looks borrowed, hastily acquired. The clothes beneath it are wrinkled and stained, carrying the dull residue of days without rest or shelter. His hair is uncombed and streaked with gray, and his beard has grown wild and uneven, as though time itself had stopped tending to him. His face is lean, the skin drawn tight over bone. His eyes are sunken but alert, exhaustion sharpened by something more rigid—defiance.

He has not bathed in days. Hunger, fear, and flight cling to him like a second skin.

Across from him stands the news anchor, upright and composed, encased in a perfectly fitted suit. His tie is precise, his shoes polished, and his hair groomed into calm symmetry.

Studio lights gleam off the glass table between them, exaggerating the distance between their worlds.

When Himmat Singh speaks, the room quiets.

"I saw Ronnie and Ashima killing Madam Riya with the vase with my own eyes," he says. "When they noticed me, Ashima told me to keep quiet. I am a poor man—only an old staff member—but I have ethics. I served the house loyally for many years."

"They tried to buy my silence," he continues. "When that failed, Ronnie chased me with the same vase to kill me. I escaped and hid in the forest."

The anchor listens without interruption, hands folded, his expression professionally neutral.

He asks, "Villa staff have stated that Madam Riya was angry that day and canceled her visit to the Gymkhana Club. All employees were given leave. Why were you still at the villa?"

Himmat Singh adjusts the shawl across his shoulders, as if steadying himself.

"When I reached my quarters," he replies, "I realized the car keys were still in my pocket. I went back to return them. That is when I saw everything."

The anchor's voice remains calm and practiced.

"If you are innocent, why didn't you approach the police? Why didn't you surrender? Why did you hide?"

Himmat Singh exhales slowly.

"That night, when the police crowd gathered," he says, "I stood outside the villa itself—wrapped in a shawl—among ordinary people. That is when I learned the police had already decided I was guilty."

"I went to Inspector Daulat's residence for help," he continues. "I told him everything. Instead, he tried to frame me. He threatened me. He said if I did not surrender, I would be killed in an encounter."

He pauses. His hands tremble slightly. His voice does not.

"I am a poor man, sir. I do not understand legal language. I believed the media was my only protection. If the police kill me, the country should know why. People must understand that the police are protecting Ronnie and Ashima. The entire system is following me."

"I want to give this full statement before a judge, without fear," he says. "And I want an investigation against Inspector Daulat. He is supporting criminals."

By law, his statement is recorded before a judicial magistrate.

Given the credible threat to his life and the allegations of police misconduct, the District Magistrate orders that

Himmat Singh was moved immediately to a guarded safe house under state protection.

The narrative fractures and reforms.

On one front, the vase is recovered.

On another, Himmat Singh steps out of silence.

It is as though time itself has rearranged the facts—the sentiments, the equations, the inevitabilities—everything recalibrated.

After a long, suffocating night, the suggestion of morning arrives quietly.

Not triumphant.

Not certain.

But unmistakably present.

37 - What Was Recovered

The courtroom was calm. Not the restless hush that precedes uncertainty, but the heavier calm that follows it—the quiet of a decision already made.

Every seat was filled. Reporters leaned forward, pens suspended, breath held not in anticipation but in confirmation.

Ronnie Grewal stood between two officers. He wore a plain shirt and slacks, posture straight, attention scattered. The clothes looked borrowed from another life—functional, anonymous, and stripped of every marker that had once made him recognizable. Damp darkened the fabric at his collar. He did not bother to smooth it.

A step behind him, Ashima Roy sat with her hands clenched in her lap, eyes fixed on the floor. The certainty she had once carried had fractured into something brittle, almost juvenile in its fear.

Near the prosecution table, Victor stood motionless.

Dr. Rosie occupied the final row reserved for expert witnesses. She wore the same coat she had worn throughout the hearings. Her file lay unopened on her knees. She had testified weeks earlier—precisely, clinically. None of it had been challenged. None of it could be. Still, her fingers worried the edge of the folder, pressing and releasing the cardboard as if testing whether it might yield.

A movement at the side entrance sent a murmur through the room.

Himmat Singh was escorted inside under police protection.

He looked smaller than memory allowed. Older. His shoulders sloped forward as though the weight of the courtroom had already settled on him. Two officers flanked him—not because he resisted, but because procedure required visibility.

Heads turned. Eyes narrowed.

Why was he here?

He was an ordinary man. A driver. A caretaker. Someone meant to fade into the margins of the case, not enter its center surrounded by scrutiny and guards.

Some faces held suspicion. Others' irritation. Did he deserve this attention? This disruption?

Himmat Singh did not look up. He stood where he was directed, hands folded, eyes lowered.

The judge acknowledged his presence without ceremony.

Himmat Singh's statement had already been entered into the record. It was brief, factual, and deliberately undramatic—constructed to endure, not to persuade.

The prosecution then addressed the recovery of the murder weapon.

The vase had been found deep in the woodland behind the property, wedged among fallen leaves and exposed roots. Dried earth clung to its base, packed into the fissures where hands had once gripped it. It was intact. Heavy. Unmistakable.

The forensic report did not speculate. It did not editorialize. It stated only that the object had been used more than once.

The judge adjusted his glasses.

Then he read.

"The prosecution has established motive, opportunity, and execution beyond reasonable doubt," he said evenly. "The court finds that the accused, Ronnie Grewal and Ashima Roy, acted with premeditation and intent."

Color drained from Ronnie's face. His lips parted as if to speak, but nothing emerged.

Ashima's shoulders trembled. Her hands tightened against her knees.

"The attempt to conceal the act as a robbery further demonstrates awareness of guilt," the judge continued. "The recovery of the murder weapon, supported by corroborating forensic evidence, leaves no room for alternate interpretation."

Dr. Rosie inhaled softly.

There was something else in her notes—an annotation she had never submitted. A marginal observation about the sequence of injuries. A possibility, not a certainty. It would not have altered the outcome. It would only have complicated it.

For a moment, she considered standing. Her hand lifted slightly from the file.

Then it fell.

Not because the science was wrong, but because she understood the cost. The court was not a place for nearly anyone. Truth, here, was not about precision. It was about closure.

The judge continued.

"This court further records its finding regarding the deliberate and aggravated cruelty inflicted upon the animal known as Leo," he said. "The evidence establishes that the injuries were purposeful and formed part of an effort to destroy potential evidence."

His gaze hardened.

"Such conduct reflects a level of moral depravity this court cannot ignore. While the sentence for the primary charge remains life imprisonment, this finding is recorded as an aggravating factor under law."

Victor's jaw tightened—not at the judgment, but at the sound of the dog's name spoken aloud.

Dr. Rosie closed her eyes briefly.

The judge turned a page.

"In the matter of the Riya Thapar murder case," he said, "this court sentences the accused, Ronnie Grewal, to life imprisonment."

A ripple passed through the courtroom before the gavel silenced it.

"Ashima Roy's sentence is deferred for a period of two years in view of her pregnancy. She is to be confined to a special women's correctional unit under judicial supervision."

At the defense table, Saamiya Siddiqui did not look at her client. She adjusted the edge of her sleeve—a precise, unconscious gesture she made only when a case was fully, irrevocably finished.

The judge spoke once more.

"Inspector Daulat Talpade is hereby placed under suspension. A separate inquiry is ordered into allegations of conspiracy to aid in the commission and concealment of the crime."

The law ended where it was required to end.

Not where the truth had begun.

Later, Ashima sat alone in a holding room while paperwork moved elsewhere.

The space was clean. Institutional. Temporary.

Her hands rested on her abdomen—not protectively, not tenderly. Measuring. Weight. Consequence.

The child was not a promise. It was evidence.

A record written into her body—binding her to a man who had already removed himself from her future.

Ronnie would leave cleanly, unburdened by continuity. She would carry forward what the court had postponed rather than spare it.

Ashima closed her eyes—not in despair, but in calculation.

This was not love. It was a liability. And knowing that did not free her. But it returned something essential. Her understanding was no longer borrowed.

38 - Too Late To Matter

The weapon was retrieved three weeks later.

It emerged without drama, without ceremony, retrieved from a dry canal bed some kilometers outside the city, wedged among mud and discarded plastic.

The glass vase was chipped and dirty, its surface damaged by exposure. The break along its base was congruent with impact.

The weight matched the injury. By the time the forensic report verified this, the discovery had already lost urgency.

Inspector Daulat analyzed the findings without an obvious reaction. The issue has moved beyond reliance on missing items.

Arrests had been made. Statements aligned. Court schedules created. The tail no longer required reinforcement.

Victor read the report twice. The evidence was significant. Belated, but solid. It would not save the case.

In court, the defense acknowledged the vase quietly. Yes, it was a viable weapon. Yes, it may have caused the damage.

But where was the chain of custody? Where was proof of possession? Why had it surfaced now after weeks of exposure, after procedural contamination?

The queries did not seek replies. They sought delay.

The judge listened. The file thickened. What arrived too late did not come at all.

Victor recognized this with astonishing clarity: truth did not perish because it was false. It expired because it missed its window of usefulness.

By the time clarity arrived, the system had already moved on.

39 - Filed Under Final (Inventory)

The case was settled in stages. Not formally at first. Not publicly.

Closure came via paperwork notations made, passages scratched out, and references removed.

The process was slow, almost delicate, as if too much finality applied at once may draw notice.

The cause of death remained unaffected. Blunt force trauma. Contributory impairment.

The phrase was specific enough to fulfill protocol and unclear enough to escape consequence. It offered a resolution without seeking permission.

Inspector Daulat signed the final register with a skilled hand. He did not pause. He did not analyze what he had previously studied. Filed under: Final.

The term communicated strength without burden. It provided finality without accountability, an ending that did not impose on believing.

Victor stood outside the courtroom as the decision was announced.

Reporters went past him, already creating headlines that

would be cemented by nightfall. Their queries were efficient. Their interest is provisional.

No one inquired about the vase. No one queried why it had taken weeks to appear.

What was crucial was that the case had reached a conclusion that could survive scrutiny, not because it was comprehensive, but because it was completed.

Victor did not feel defeated. He felt guided. This was how endings were formed.

The items were processed discreetly. White hands moved from thing to item, never staying long enough to indicate remembrance.

No ceremony. No relatives present. Just officials, ledgers, and a long table where things were inserted one by one, given values, and then meaning.

Clothes first. Then papers. Then jewelry. When they neared the jewels, the inventory officer hesitated. "This one was photographed earlier," he said. "But it's not here now." The assistant examined the list.

The officer made a notation in the margin. Item unaccounted for. Status: unresolved. He adjusted his specs and continued on. He did not circle it. Unresolved did not compel action. Only acknowledgment. The file moved on.

40 - The Version That Finalized

By morning, the headlines had settled. The press version stabilized quickly.

A renowned businesswoman. A troubled marriage. Financial strain. A robbery gone wrong, sharpened by personal betrayal.

The language was efficient and confident—built for repetition rather than understanding. Early reports hedged. Later ones did not. Timelines were simplified. Motives aligned.

Contradictions were labeled under investigation until they disappeared from follow-up coverage, replaced by summaries that required no qualification. Details that resisted coherence were minimized. The missing staff member became a logistical footnote. The delayed recovery of the weapon was framed as routine.

Procedural disruptions were attributed to backlog and process. Expert panels filled the gaps—former officers, legal analysts, and psychologists each offering interpretation where facts thinned. Speculation hardened into explanation, repeated until it lost its conditional tone.

Riya Thapar was remembered selectively: powerful, demanding, and isolated. Her death was framed as tragic but foreseeable—the cost of ambition and exposure. Sympathy was permitted only within limits that did not disturb the narrative.

Ronnie blurred. Ashima receded. Complexity was reduced to usefulness. The case was no longer active. It was informative. Public memory adjusted.

What could not be confirmed was overtaken by what could be conveyed. Each circulation generated its own verification. The press version did not mislead. It concluded.

What survived existed elsewhere—in fragments: private recollections, unsigned documents, incidents never recorded because no one had asked at the right moment, or because asking would have required a different kind of attention than the moment allowed.

Naina read the coverage from her hotel room. She noticed what was absent more than what remained: the softened edges, the missing hours.

The city absorbed the narrative and moved around it. The case became something that had happened, not something still unfolding. The version that survived did not ask to be believed. It only needed to remain.

41 - A Victory That Didn't Belong

Victor Banerjee was now the talk of the town.

He wore the same jacket to every presentation now. No one commented on it.

Everyone noticed. Everyone knew how he had solved the case and how neatly the facts had unfolded under his fingers.

Even the judge had acknowledged him in open court, a quick nod that conveyed more than applause.

That evening, Victor sat alone at a roadside tea stall near the police station, staring into nothing in particular.

Steam rose from the kettle and fogged his glasses. He authorized it. For a minute longer than needed, he did not clean them.

"Victor, sir, one tea from my side," the chaiwala said.

Victor accepted the glass and held it gingerly, the warmth registering late, if at all.

Not for the first time, he thought about whether he had solved the case or twisted it so it may survive.

The praises had come effortlessly. Too easy. It had advanced faster than skeptics ever did.

In the newspaper, his name appeared with phrases like "clarity," "resolve," and "precision."

The city needs a figure to keep the finale in place. Victor had filled out the form without resistance.

He watched the tea cool without tasting it. Truth, he believed, needs moderation.

What scared him now was not guilt. It was recognition.

The triumph was complete. Nothing about him appeared victorious. It was not clean.

He gulped the tea and stood. Victor moved away from the stall without looking back.

42 - The Last Unsent Letter

Victor sat at the desk without turning on the light.

The desk lamp sat within reach, its switch familiar, worn smooth by habit. He left it untouched. Darkness felt appropriate. Honest.

His sleeves were rolled unevenly—one higher than the other.

He noticed it, registered it, and decided not to correct it. It did not matter.

The notebook lay open before him. The first page had already been torn away. The second waited, pale and blank. A pen rested beside it, aligned with unnecessary precision, as if order alone might substitute for resolution.

He wrote her name once.

Rosie.

The ink bled slightly into the paper. He lingered at the curve of the R longer than necessary, then struck a line through it.

The second attempt came more slowly.

Dr. Panicker.

Too formal. Too distant. Too controlled. He crossed that out as well.

On the third attempt, he did not begin with her name.

You are the only person I know who would not mistake this for remorse.

There are things the file does not disclose.

He paused. Read the sentence again. Then again. It sounded defensive. Like justification masquerading as transparency. Like a man already preparing his own defense. He scratched it out.

The room was quiet.

Outside the window, a car passed at a distance, its tires hissing briefly against damp asphalt before the sound dissolved.

The quiet settled back into place.

He began again.

This time, he did not stop.

I am writing this knowing you may never read it.

That knowledge may be the only reason I can continue.

I am writing to you because you understand how damage is assembled. You understand sequence. You know that once events are placed in order, intention becomes irrelevant.

I was not born this way. Somewhere along the way, I changed.

It did not happen all at once. There was no single moment of collapse. There were adjustments. Small accommodations.

Decisions that felt reasonable when taken in isolation and inevitable when viewed in retrospect.

I never respected women. I did not think of it as hatred. I thought of it as a hierarchy. Women existed beneath us—objects to be used, leveraged, and enjoyed. Naked things are meant for access rather than regard. This belief formed slowly, reinforced by success and silence, by the absence of consequence.

It shaped everything that followed.

The photographs.

The delays.

The silences.

The transactions.

None of it felt like betrayal at the time. It felt like management. I learned to grow around certain facts. The same instincts that made me effective also made me dangerous.

I once believed corruption announced itself loudly. I was wrong. It arrives quietly, dressed as logic. As duty. As responsibility.

What I called interrogation was, in truth, blackmail.

My work with Riya began as curiosity. She wanted answers. I gave her competence. A private investigation into Ronnie and Ashima—quiet, contained, efficient. At first, it felt clean. Surveillance. Verification. Pattern-building. I told myself I was still operating within acceptable limits.

Money changed that.

According to the records, Hotel Hilltop had been bleeding quietly for years. A loss-making property. A recurring deficit. Riya spoke of it as an inconvenience—something that demanded attention without offering return.

I saw opportunity and enjoyed the symmetry of it.

I proposed a conversion. In exchange for the investigation I had conducted into Ronnie and Ashima, she would gift me the hotel.

My intention was not preservation. It was a transformation.

I planned to convert the property into a high-end singing-and-dancing bar. Such places were always in demand. They attracted tourists—especially groups of men—and generated predictable revenue. My ambition extended further: to elevate prostitution into a premium tier, curated and discreet, insulated by access and price.

I believed degradation could be refined if packaged correctly.

Before that future could be secured, my corruption deepened.

Riya had been using drugs long before any of this. I became her source. I knew when to provide and when to conceal. She trusted me because I calibrated her need.

Once, at Hotel Hilltop, she overdosed. She was disoriented. Barely conscious.

I took advantage of her.

I photographed her in that state—nude, compromised. At the time, I told myself it was insurance. Evidence. Foresight. Containment. I convinced myself truth without control was useless.

I was playing a double game, and I enjoyed the balance it required.

In the name of investigation, I began blackmailing Ashima as well. Compromised photographs. Carefully timed pressure. Ronnie could not protect her. I exploited that gap deliberately.

Ashima's pregnancy—what I thought would secure my leverage—escaped my control. What I believed was contained became public. What I believed was mine to deploy was taken from me without effort.

By then, I had embedded myself deeply into the larger arrangement forming around Riya. Not out of loyalty. Out of calculation. Another attempt to extract relevance—money, leverage, survival. I believed there was profit to be made by staying close to damage.

But Ronnie, Ashima, Saamiya, and Daulat were already a unit. Closed. They used me where convenient and excluded me where it mattered.

Had they brought me fully inside, things might have ended differently. I might have protected them. I might have secured something for myself.

Instead, I remained at the margins—useful, expendable, replaceable.

Daulat's plan was elegant. Approved by Ronnie. Accepted by Ashima. Everything was to begin at eleven.

Riya's drink would be altered moments before the argument. Alcohol. Stress. A collapse that could later be explained. The drug came from Daulat. Ronnie delivered it.

In return, Daulat was promised a guided investigation—one whose conclusion could be shaped.

That was the elegance of the arrangement. I understand now that elegance is often harm made orderly enough to escape protest.

What none of us knew—and what I discovered too late—was that Riya had already moved first.

Her estate had been restructured quietly, cleanly, and legally. Every significant holding now rested with Desai & Associates.

By the time we believed we were acting, we were already irrelevant.

At eleven fifteen, I entered the villa. I wore gloves.

Riya was seated upright on the couch. Her dog, Leo—a brown Labrador—watched me closely. Alert. Uncertain.

She asked for her belongings first. I handed her the package. I told her it was a gift. I said I was glad. My voice did not change.

I placed the folder on the table—photographs of Ronnie and Ashima. I told her the investigation was complete. I said this fulfilled our agreement.

I also presented the gift deed for Hotel Hilltop. She skimmed it and set it aside.

She refused.

She said she would transfer the property on one condition.

She asked me to assassinate Ronnie.

I refused—not because the accusation was false, but because it exceeded my mandate.

She said there would be no hotel.

I showed her what I had kept from the past. Her own photographs. Her compromised body. I reminded her of the documents I possessed—shell companies, diversions, and tax arrangements that would not survive daylight.

Among them, I concealed a supplementary authorization.

She signed without reading.

I thanked her. I said goodbye.

As I left, she cursed me.

She turned toward the dog. Leo lunged. I ran.

The dog cornered me, barking, frightened. I sprayed him once—non-lethally. He collapsed behind the bushes.

As I crossed the border walk, I felt it.

Not pursuit.

Not confrontation.

Being seen.

I believed Himmat Singh stood watching from the dark line of trees beyond the eastern wall. I had no proof. No sound confirmed it.

By the time I reached the road, certainty had narrowed into possibility.

Himmat Singh would later disclose nothing about that night. Which means either he saw nothing—or he chose not to see.

That is why I wanted to find him first.

Not out of concern.

Out of fear.

I feared he would place me where I was never meant to exist.

Silence, in the wrong hands, becomes accusation.

By eleven thirty, I was gone.

Later that night, Riya died.

When the news reached me, I returned. The villa was chaos.

Only later did the structure emerge.

The poison came first.

The vase ended it.

Once the death was declared murder, Hotel Hilltop became unreachable. The estate transfer was legal. Final. Irreversible.

Still, something disturbed me.

Not the plan.

Not the timing.

Not even the lie.

But the possibility that the truth had been fully witnessed and never spoken.

For the first time, I breathed freely when, in the statement, Himmat Singh mentioned nothing. Not my presence. Not my departure. Not my involvement.

Whether he saw nothing or chose not to see no longer mattered.

What mattered was that my name never entered the record.

And yet, I was the greatest loser.

I assumed Riya would die quietly and that Hotel Hilltop would come to me without notice. I never imagined her death would be staged into a spectacle.

They destroyed every expectation I had constructed. They dismantled my ambitions with precision.

My expertise failed me. My calculations collapsed.

Afterward, suspicion settled into everything.

Naina Talwar's timing is exact. Her silences are placed.

Isha Diwan is far too quiet. Silence of that kind is never empty. It is held.

Too many people wear masks. It is impossible to know who is innocent and who is merely waiting.

Some nights the impulse is simple: I want to kill them all with my own hands. Not strategically. Not cleanly. Just to end the uncertainty.

I do nothing.

Not because I cannot—but because restraint is the last form of control left to me.

Only then did my past with you reassert itself fully.

I never loved you. Perhaps that is why our marriage ended in divorce. When I learned you had joined forensics, I burned with jealousy. Your legitimacy exposed my fraudulence.

That night, when we crossed the border, it was calculated. I needed you, and I used you. Ashima and Riya were gone. You were present, willing, tested, and available.

There was no love in it.

Only advantage.

The surge of energy you felt was nothing more than drugs. I knew this.

Compelled by habit, I photographed you—nude, without consent. I told myself the images might be useful someday.

How far I have fallen.

For a while, my name circulated. People whispered it. They called me sharp. Dangerous. Effective.

But admiration does not sustain a household.

Applause does not pay bills.

Recognition buys, at best, a cup of tea from a street vendor.

A life does not run on appreciation.

It runs on money.

And I was left with none.

Not the pension.

Not the exit.

Not the future.

My conscience is dead. I am nothing but a living corpse.

I did not cross a line.

I designed it.

Victor stopped.

The pen hovered above the page, suspended between ink and limit. At last, he placed it down—carefully, parallel to the edge of the desk—and closed the notebook.

He did not tear the page out.

He did not destroy it.

He left it there, folded within the pad.

Unfinished.

43 - A Closed Body

Victor broke down. There was nothing left that made sense. His retirement plan was in ruins; the future he had methodically projected shattered to ash. With no one to blame and nowhere left to run, Victor overdosed on drugs and ended his life.

The act itself was unceremonious. No note was left in plain sight. No gesture is designed for interpretation. Only the sequence was precise, deliberate, and congruent with the way he had lived.

The body was discovered hours later, already cooled into stillness, the settings around it neat enough to reflect intent rather than impulse. Inspector Sujoy Ghosh assumed responsibility for the case. He was present at the scene when Victor was found dead.

The room was quiet, but the weight of defeat weighed on every surface—papers laid too neatly, a chair pushed in too far, and the subtle chemical residue that persisted in the air long after the tablets had done their work.

Ghosh moved into the gap gingerly. Too cautiously. He examined Victor's possessions without hurry.

Inside the bag, he found countless packets of drugs, enough to narrate everything if explanation was all that was required. He noticed the site. The amount. The ease with which the plot developed itself.

Suicide would be easy. A guy in hardship. A prominent detective is exposed to closeness with corruption. A decrease from significance. The narrative wrote itself.

Ghosh's hand paused at the desk. Inside a folder, he found the letter for Rosie. Folded perfectly. Aligned at the corners. Placed where discovery would appear inevitable but controlled.

Beneath it was another paper from Hotel Hilltop bearing Riya's signature, deadlines adjusted just enough to matter, and approval disguised within otherwise regular papers.

Ghosh read without expression. What Victor had left behind was not chaos. It was a sequence. The confession did not plead. It did not justify. It accepted acts without show and responsibility without explanation. It was not written to be read publicly. It was written to be handled. Ghosh noticed that quickly.

He closed the folder. Then, without hesitation, he started to deconstruct it. The confession letter was removed first.

The Hotel Hilltop document followed. He separated pages, altered their arrangement, and amended portions of the preliminary report to maintain consistency when absence would thereafter be acknowledged. The papers were incinerated. Not completely, never completely, but broken to pieces, edges scorched beyond recognition.

Enough to ensure nothing readable remains. Enough to make rehabilitation worthless. By the time the room was fixed, the table was already set.

Inspector Ghosh completed the paperwork slowly.

The body had been accounted for. The cause was documented. The case, formally speaking, was finished. Closure had been achieved without disruption.

He had not joined the police to be brave. He had joined because he believed in the method.

As a young officer, he had trusted rigor. He believed airtight cases could force the system to stand by truth. For a while, it worked. He solved cases others avoided. Seniors called him sharp. Juniors believed he proved honesty could survive inside the force.

That illusion ended when his investigations began pointing upward. Files were reassigned. Witnesses withdrew. Transfers arrived disguised as promotions.

Each time, Ghosh adjusted. He believed persistence would outlast resistance. Then came the case that taught him otherwise.

A death that resisted explanation. Political proximity. Medical contradictions. He pursued it carefully. Legally. By the book.

The pressure was subtle. An informant vanished. A junior was suspended. His wife received a polite warning. No one told him to stop. They isolated him instead.

The case was dismantled legally and impeccably. Evidence insufficient. Motives are speculative. Responsibility diffused across committees. No one is guilty. Everyone is correct.

For the first time, Ghosh bent procedure. Pressured a witness. Skipped a safeguard. Not for gain but for closure.

It made no difference. The case collapsed anyway. That was when he understood. The system could absorb honesty and compromise equally without consequence. Righteousness only made you visible. And visibility was the real offense.

After that, he chose smaller cases. Clean ones. Weightless ones. He became reliable. Unremarkable.

People assumed he had grown afraid. They were wrong. Ghosh had learned where courage failed to scale. He signed the final page and closed the file.

Some things, he knew, were buried not because they were forgotten but because remembering them changed nothing.

At Ghosh's request, Dr. Rosie Panicker was contacted about Victor's death. She had already reached the airport. Her baggage was checked. Her boarding pass was generated.

The officers came to the airport and asked her to leave with them. She did not ask questions. She turned back, not as a forensic officer. She had already accomplished that role, but for reasons she did not study deeply.

Some findings did not require explanation. The body lay still beneath the white sheet. The stare no longer carried intention, just consequence.

When Rosie saw Victor for the first time, the room faded away. She remembered the night she had longed to stay. The unopened bottle. The file closed between them.

The alternative she had presented as discipline, as duty. Work had interfered. It always did. She remembered the way he had sighed softly as she departed. Not in rage. In understanding. The recollections strike now with the weight of finality. This was the closure she had not recognized; she was postponing it.

It came on her face, not as agony, but knowledge. The awareness that some endings happen not because of what was done, but because of what was delayed too long. She stood there just a bit longer. Then she stepped back.

The autopsy determined that Victor had died of a heart attack. Not suicide. Ghosh did not want Victor's recently regained reputation to be tainted by scandal. The system has already utilized him. There was no need to trash him publicly.

But Rosie felt uneasy. Not by the body. By the room. The absence of something that should have been there. The excessive order. The way certain locations appeared cleansed rather than unoccupied.

She could not articulate what was missing, only that something had been removed intentionally. Across the hallway was Naina's room. She may have been an eyewitness. But before the detectives could interrogate her, Naina checked out early the next morning. She left without a trace. Victor's body was liberated.

The case was closed. And Rosie, having taken one last peek at what could no longer be changed, returned to work.

It was the only site that remained where emotion could be postponed without consequence. Or so she told herself. Some truths, she recognized, did not need to be articulated. They only needed to be carried.

44 - The Registration

The guest registration sat open on the counter. Hotel Hilltop did not utilize computers for such things yet. Names were written by hand, dates were marked in blue ink, and rooms were presented in a clean, professional way.

The register itself was heavy, with a fractured spine from years of frequent use. Owners, renovations, and unjustified policy changes have all survived.

The cashier ran his finger down the page. His nail hooked briefly in the paper's grain, then moved on.

Talwar, Naina

Room 214

Check-in: 31st December of 1997

Check-out: 29th January of 1998

He hesitated. There was a little indentation above the name from the pressure of writing that had been erased. Not crossed out. Rubbed away. The paper there was thinner, weakened by correction. He adjusted the paper slightly, letting the above light catch it. Another name had previously been there. Shorter. The shape lingered in the grain of the paper, incomplete but deliberate.

Whoever had removed it had done it carefully enough to eliminate the data, but not enough to ruin the paper. This was not panic. It's a revision. The clerk hesitated. Registers were not evidence. They were convenient. They existed to ease travel, not to retain reality.

What could yet be read was more significant than what had already been written. He looked at the indentation once again. There were no instructions for this case. No process for names that have opted not to remain. Slowly, he closed the register. The sound it created wasn't pleasant.

Finally enough. He put the register back into its spot beneath the counter, aligning it with the others. The shelf was already full. Space has never been an issue. Memory had. If a name was gone, it was gone. And if it had never been written properly to begin with, there was nothing to retrieve. The clerk straightened the counter, put the pen near the register, and called out to the following guest.

Part VI

Aftermath

45 - What Was Carried Away

The same morning, Naina sat by the window seat of the taxi as it went toward the airport. Her reflection slid over the glass—faint, fractured, unrecognizable.

Leo slept near her, quieter than usual, breathing steadily. Alive. The discharge papers waited in her bag, signed and stamped. Custody had shifted without dispute.

She told herself she had rescued him. She did not examine what that claim still required.

Vikram sat in the front seat, relaxed and serene. He possessed the attitude of someone whose war was finished, whose dangers had already been etched into history.

The calm between them was operational, not unpleasant. It bore the weight of finished steps, not plans in preparation.

Nothing needed to be mentioned because nothing needed to be discussed anymore. She had carried the knowledge instead, allowing it to settle into something colder than bitterness and more persistent than wrath.

The city dwindled into a road. Vikram stated once. "Madam, the estate filings will be completed soon," he observed.

"There will be no discretionary delays."

After a long time, Naina felt astonishingly light. Naina nodded. She did not query how. She did not need to. Insurance, wills, and contingency clauses—these were not conversations.

Vikram spoke in a low voice. "The self-drive car you took was the one from the local tours-and-travels company. The accident. It's been handled."

He paused. "Accounts settled. Quietly"

Naina nodded again.

They were sequences already in action. What mattered today was not intention but follow-through. She believed she had done what was necessary. The notion did not settle.

When Naina closed her eyes, the night of December 31st did not return as a remembrance. It returned as a sequence. Not horror, but order.

She was, in truth, Tina Desaithe, the concealed owner of Desai & Associates. The name has always existed; it had merely waited for space. Naina Talwar was the name that survived. Tina Desai was the one who remembered.

One thing goes to the next without interruption or debate. Tina, Riya, and Isha grew up believing they were inseparable. Their childhood was stitched together by laughter, secrets, and a shared certainty that adulthood would bring freedom, not ruin.

Their families were bound just as closely. Mr. Thapar and Mr. Diwan were business partners, while Tina's father, Mr. Desai, served as their meticulous lawyer and trusted friend. Himmat Singh, their driver, was a quiet constant in their lives. He drove them everywhere, letting them eat ice cream before lunch, taking long routes just to hear them laugh. Riya always sat in front, restless and commanding. Tina and Isha sat behind, arguing about dreams. Himmat never learned to lie; his loyalty was instinctive, unquestioned.

Even then, the imbalance was present. Riya grew up without a mother, cocooned in wealth and her father's excessive indulgence. She studied in Palankhet itself, never separated from Mr. Thapar, never denied anything. The sheltering did not strengthen her; it sharpened her need for control. Tina and Isha, by contrast, were sent to a boarding school outside Palankhet. Distance gave them discipline. Tina learned independence early, shaping her life on her own terms. Isha learned silence, observation, and endurance.

Though Tina and Riya were close, Riya's dominance always existed beneath the friendship. Power mattered to her, even in affection. When Tina found special love, Riya crossed an unacceptable line. Not out of passion, but out of control. She interfered deliberately, bringing anguish to the person Tina loved, knowing that indirect harm would cut deeper.

It was not a single incident. Again and again, Riya intruded wherever Tina found joy, compelled to destroy what she herself could never own. Tina lived freely; Riya never had that freedom. Wealth had sheltered her, not prepared her. In that imbalance, jealousy hardened into resentment.

After completing their studies, Tina and Isha planned to pursue their master's degrees in the U.S. Isha's marks prevented her from going, but she encouraged Tina without hesitation. Tina left for the U.S., unaware that her life was about to fracture permanently.

During her studies, she met with a brutal car accident. Her mother was with her in the car. Tina survived but slipped into a deep coma. Her mother did not.

From the beginning, Mr. Desai believed the crash was not accidental. He suspected intent and knew visibility would endanger Tina further. To protect her, he made an unthinkable choice.

The world was told Tina Desai had died.

Officially erased. Legally nonexistent. Tina Desai became Naina Talwar. Only Isha and Himmat Singh knew the truth.

In reality, she lived quietly in the United States, undergoing long-term treatment under her new name. Naina Talwar remained in a coma for three years.

While she lay unconscious, the world did not pause. Trust hardened into authority, and authority into theft. One family vanished without documentation. Mr. Desai spent nearly everything to keep her alive. His wealth disappeared first. His health followed.

Three years later, Naina woke up.

Recovery was long and punishing. It took seven full months for her body and mind to regain strength. During that time, she learned the truth about the accident, Riya's involvement in her accident, her mother's death, and her new identity. Anger did not erupt. It settled. Quiet. Enduring.

By the time Naina was strong enough to return to the world, Mr. Desai could no longer run his firm. His health had deteriorated beyond repair. He handed over Desai & Associates to his daughter. Naina accepted the responsibility with discipline and restraint. Outwardly, she rebuilt order. Inwardly, rage waited with patience.

As the computer age reshaped business, Naina launched a software-based consultancy, positioning herself where real power now lived—inside systems, data, and silence.

She did not build the venture alone. She partnered with Salim, the son of Suleman Uncle, whose charm masked a sharp, calculating mind.

Where Naina remained invisible, Salim negotiated openly. He impressed Riya with promises of modernization and efficiency, framing digitization as progress rather than intrusion. Riya approved the contracts without suspicion. Through Salim, access was secured to her office, her villa, and her private world.

Quietly, Naina monitored everything. The transition was seamless. Invisible. Gradually, fragments surfaced—private communications, discreet financial movements. Every message Riya had ever sent to Victor lay open before her. If Victor knew much, Naina knew far more. With each discovery, resentment deepened, aged, darkened, and sharpened by time.

Then the final truth emerged. Inspector Daulat, corrupt by habit, not ambition, Ronnie, and Ashima were planning Riya's quiet death was an ending designed to raise no suspicion. Once Riya was gone, control of the Thapar estate would pass entirely to Ronnie. Naina saw the symmetry and smiled. With a single act, she could dismantle their conspiracy and settle her own score.

Riya was her prey. And Riya's end would belong to her alone.

So Naina began to plan.

Naina would remember December with uncomfortable precision. Staying in Palankhet. Being seen without being approached. Letting fear build its own momentum. There had been notes. Typed. Always the same words. Fear did not require variation.

Riya had kept one. Folded it. Given another away, as if evidence could intervene where meaning had failed. The typewriter had never been brought inside the house. That had mattered.

Himmat had understood distance. How to be seen without being recognized. How memory could be impersonated more effectively than flesh.

What Riya called spirits were only silhouettes arranged for her guilt to inhabit.

Isha had understood access. Timing. Silence. None of them had planned for contact. That was the mistake.

Riya had sealed the rooms. Taken the pills. Trusted the quiet. She had waited for something she could no longer understand. They had wanted her to see. She never did.

Naina arrived at the villa without warning. Not to expose the plot but to end it herself. Not merely to kill Riya, but to claim the conclusion she believed had always been hers.

The past had come full circle. Retribution was no longer an idea. It was inevitable.

By the time she came to the villa, hesitation had already faded. There were limits plain enough, at least then.

At eleven fifty-six, Naina entered the house wearing a black hoodie, unmarked, precisely selected, its silhouette intentional rather than apparent.

The material absorbed light—restrained, practical, and forgettable. She did not remove it immediately.

Riya was alone on the couch when Naina sauntered into the living room.

Riya had been awake for hours, though she could not say when sleep had ended.

Time no longer behaved reliably. It stretched, folded back on itself, and repeated without sequence. The room was quiet in the way she had demanded it to be sealed, padded, and protected from intrusion. The silence pressed inward, heavy and incomplete.

She was inhaling white powder, her breath erratic enough to distribute it across the table. The spark of wonder disappeared instantly, replaced by irritation.

Ronnie and Ashima remained upstairs, precisely where they had been earlier. A dull thud sounded overhead—footsteps shifting, not approaching, but real enough to remind the house it was occupied.

Riya's breathing came unevenly. Each inhale felt negotiated, as though the body required persuasion to continue.

She sensed the presence before she opened her eyes.

It was always like this. Not sudden. Not dramatic. A certainty arriving without announcement.

Riya kept her eyes shut.

If she did not look, it would not be real.

That had always worked before.

Her breathing scraped in her chest, shallow and uneven. The powder on the table lay disturbed, half-smeared, its symmetry broken by her hand. She tasted metal at the back of her throat.

A presence stood near her. Not sudden. Not loud. Certain.

"Tina," she whispered. The name came out wrong, flattened, softened by fear until it meant nothing at all. "Please."

No answer.

The silence stretched. It did not recede.

When she opened her eyes, the figure was closer than she expected. Too close for a hallucination. Too still for comfort.

But the face did not settle.

Fear rearranged iterated details and smoothed edges. She saw not a person but an outline, a consequence without form.

Naina watched her.

This was the moment she had carried for years. The moment was supposed to land clean, unmistakable, and final.

It didn't.

Riya wasn't looking at her.

She was looking through her.

"No," Naina said quietly.

She reached forward and gripped Riya's face, her fingers digging in, forcing her head upright. Thumbs pressed into soft skin until it hurt.

"Look at me."

Riya flinched, eyes squeezing shut again, as if darkness were still a refuge.

"I know," she said breathlessly. "I know why you're here."

But she didn't.

The apology was misdirected. The guilt belonged to someone safer. Someone is already dead. Something in Naina shifted.

Not rage. Not triumph. The understanding that recognition would never come.

Her gaze dropped, not to Riya but to the table beside them.

The vase stood there. Clear glass. Heavy. Blue floral embossing rose beneath her fingers even before she touched it. She had noticed it earlier and dismissed it. Decorative. Harmless.

Now it waited. She told herself she would not. Her hand closed around it before the thought finished forming.

The movement was wrong—too fast, too unconsidered. Thought lagged behind muscle. The arc was imperfect and unplanned.

The impact landed with a sound that did not belong in memory—dense, muted, and final.

Riya screamed. The vase did not break. Naina froze. This was not what she had come to do.

For a fraction of a timeless second, the world stalled, as if offering revision. Then someone else moved.

Isha had been standing there all along.

Her hands closed around the vase. The raised blue pattern scraped her skin as she lifted it. She did not look at Naina. She did not hesitate.

The blows came without rhythm, without counting, without mercy.

Not punishment. Interruption. Termination.

Riya's body gave way quickly. The fear had done most of the work long before this moment.

When it ended, there was no clarity. Only stillness where resistance had been.

What Riya carried with her when she died was fear—unresolved, misdirected, and complete.

It had never found its proper object. It had never reached the truth. It simply ended dense and unspent.

Silence rushed back in, thicker now, poisoned. Fireworks detonated outside. Midnight arrived unnoticed.

Isha's breath broke. Not a cry—something sharper. Her hands shook as they closed around the vase. The blue floral embossing tore at her skin, but she did not loosen her grip. She struck as if stopping something already too late.

Naina did not stop her immediately. She stood still. Whether the calm was astonishment or allowance became harder to define later.

Isha collapsed inward, apologies and old humiliations spilling between breaths. Naina recognized the expression.

She had worn it once. Long before this night.

When Naina spoke, her voice held.

"Enough. You shouldn't be here. This is dangerous."

Her gaze dropped to Isha's clothes, darkened beyond repair.

"Get rid of them," Naina said. "If you're seen like this, it ends."

Isha nodded immediately.

"Leave the villa," Naina continued. "I'll handle the rest."

Fear, Naina knew, could be counted on.

She took the vase with her. Transparent glass, the blue floral embossing still raised beneath her fingers. It disappeared without a sound.

As Naina reached the outer walkway, someone stepped out of the darkness.

Himmat Singh.

He did not raise his voice. He did not ask questions. He looked once at the clear glass vase, the blue floral embossing unmarred, and understood everything.

"This wasn't part of the plan," he murmured. "Go. Get away from the villa."

For a moment, Naina didn't move.

"You shouldn't be here like this," he added. "This will swallow you."

She searched his face for calculation, for betrayal. There was none.

Only the same steadiness she remembered from childhood.

Naina ran.

Driving away, another fear surfaced, and with it, the memory of why she had returned to the villa at all. The car accident had not been an error. It had been intentional. A calculated disruption meant to place her back inside the sequence, to justify her presence, and to realign timing.

Isha was shaken. Shaken people misstepped. Panic lingered. Evidence survived intention.

The plan had accounted for distance, not fracture.

Naina turned back.

Returning now was not deviation. It was containment. Leaving would have created witnesses.

At twelve fifteen a.m., the villa stood silent. Clean.

Isha had followed instructions perfectly.

Naina was no longer outside the sequence.

Staying required less justification than leaving. The machinery took over.

When the officers came and began questioning, staying required less justification than leaving. The concept of stealing took shape simply. She adjusted to it. Across the room, Isha noticed her and went rigid.

Naina caught her gaze and put a finger to her lips. Silence was no longer an option.

When Isha handed Naina the black coffee, both of them finally breathed a sigh of relief.

Vikram's visit to the property with the insurance paperwork and the alleged new will was no coincidence. It, too, had been precisely arranged by Naina. The objective was straightforward: to guarantee that Ronnie could be imprisoned beyond escape in the wake of Riya's death.

In reality, the will had never been altered. That deception was effortless for Naina, a mere exercise of skill. Riya's signatures were scattered throughout every corner of her office, preserved in files and drafts accumulated over years. And if a lawyer did not exploit such advantages, who ever would?

The insurance documents, however, were authentic. It was this small, legal, and undeniable detail that would ultimately seal his fate.

The taxi joined the highway.

Morning light constricted the city's limits, ignorant of what had been removed overnight.

Behind her, a house empty of reality. Ahead, distance.

She looked briefly at Leo.

Some things did not loosen their hold when one was gone or because one survived.

What Naina and Isha carried away was not relief.

It was the knowledge that truth, when it arrives too late, does not redeem anything.

It only leaves a body behind.

What was carried away was not revenge. It was a consequence.

And the consequence, once lifted, did not ask where it was being taken.

46 - After Silence

The cab drew to a stop at the exit gate. Before the engine had fully died, Naina was already reaching for the door.

Vikram leaned forward to pay the driver, while Leo stepped out to retrieve the baggage. Naina scarcely noticed any of them.

Isha was standing near the glass doors. Her clothes were clean today but worn thin. She hadn't changed much, still elegant and constantly watchful, but there was something tighter in her position now, something solidified.

When Naina spotted her, a smile burst through the tiredness on her face. She crossed the space between them and pulled Isha into a powerful, wordless hug.

For a moment, they simply held each other. It felt like victory. Not the boisterous, winning kind but the peaceful certainty that comes when a long duty has finally begun to be repaid.

The kind that does not proclaim itself, because it needs no witnesses. A remembrance surfaced then, uninvited and accurate.

Back outside the terminal, Naina drew back and put a folded document into Isha's palm.

"The photocopies," she said gently. "Thapar estate papers."

Isha looked down at them, then back up.

"Give it one month," Naina continued, her voice steady. "That estate will be Diwan's again."

Isha's fingers curled around the pages. Her eyes shimmered, but she didn't cry. She didn't anymore.

Naina reached into her bag and placed something else in Isha's hand—a small, newly engraved nameplate. The metal caught the light. DIWAN'S VILLA. Isha stared at it, breath caught somewhere between disbelief and memory.

"Keep it," Naina said softly. "You'll need it soon."

They hugged again, longer this time. Then, inevitably, they let go.

As Naina stepped back, her tone changed—not colder, but resolute. "Because of my health, I couldn't complete my master's," she said. "You must do it. For yourself. And for me. Education matters now more than ever."

Isha nodded slowly, clutching the papers and the nameplate to her chest. The promise was already forming in her silence.

Naina turned away without another word. Some things no longer needed saying.

Naina's voice faltered for the first time.

"If I hadn't gone into that coma," she said quietly, "you wouldn't have had to endure so much. I couldn't protect Diwan Uncle. I couldn't save your mother. I did nothing for them. I'm sorry." She paused, choosing her words carefully. "What they were forced to live through—they never deserved any of it."

Isha shook her head, her expression steady but tired.

"I failed you too," she replied. "I couldn't help you when you needed it most. I didn't even have enough money to come see you in the U.S." Her voice softened. "We were both helpless, Naina. That wasn't a choice; it was fate."

For a moment, neither of them spoke. The silence carried grief, forgiveness, and a shared understanding that blame no longer had a place between them.

"That night," Naina commented softly, "I underestimated you. I assumed you were weak and that you wouldn't be able to handle the case." She hesitated. "That fear is why I came back."

Isha shook her head. "No. I knew you'd come back. Because you can't leave me alone."

A slight grin went between them. "And anyway," Naina added, "you cleaned the evidence very carefully."

"This is my everyday work," Isha said. "And I'm good at it." She stopped, then continued, her voice lower. "But the way you handled things—if that object had been found, it would've been stressful for all of us."

Isha paused. "And Victor...?"

Naina's expression shifted, not abruptly, but enough to register. A tightening. A shadow passing through.

Isha hesitated, then spoke, her voice low, almost embarrassed by its urgency.

"I was terrified," Isha said quietly. "That day, when Victor came to your quarter."

She drew a breath. "I was shaking inside. He saw our photograph on the wall. He kept staring at it. I didn't know what to say. I didn't dare react. I just asked him to leave."

Her voice tightened. "There was something wrong in his eyes. The way he looked at my chest while talking so openly, so shamelessly. It was horrible. He wasn't even trying to hide it. He's a rascal." The words landed hard.

Naina's face drained of color. Her jaw clenched, fingers curling into her palm until her knuckles whitened. Her eyes flushed, not with tears, but with rage.

"That's why he didn't get to live," Naina said flatly.

She drew a breath, steady but cold. “He came into my room last night high on drugs, rambling nonsense. He threatened me. Tried to take advantage of me.” Her lips pressed into a thin line. “I kicked him where it hurt most. He screamed and ran back to his room.”

A pause.

“Drugs had already hollowed him out,” she said. “I just made sure there was no way back.” Her voice did not rise. It hardened. “I kept kicking him again and again until he stopped responding.”

Isha froze. Then, quietly, “Did you... kill him?"

Naina raised her hand.

“Don’t ask that.”

She didn’t look away. She didn’t explain.

Isha nodded. She didn’t ask again. Isha studied her face. Naina did not look away, but she offered nothing more. The atmosphere seemed to reset into stillness.

Himmat Singh stood at the entrance. Seeing Naina, he greeted her with folded hands. Not as a suspect. Not as a caretaker. As Driver Uncle.

Isha answered, "Driver Uncle hid the vase as soon as you left the villa." "He calmed me down, told me not to be scared, and said I might not see him for a few days."

Himmat said quietly, "There will be a lot of misunderstanding, and many hypotheses will come up, but don't worry. God will give you strength, my girl."

Himmat stood quietly; his eyes fell. "Driver Uncle has grown old," Naina remarked softly, "but what a miracle he pulled off. I felt he wouldn't support us." She added, "With Vikram's help, I sent Ashima the note in her tiffin box and Victor the location of the vase."

"And I sent Driver Uncle to the media." Isha said.

"At the perfect time," Naina continued, "he showed amazing courage." "The performance he put on for the media was remarkable. "Almost theatrical if it hadn't been real."

Isha said again, her voice lower. "They were brave." Naina did not refute her. "Himmat Singh raised his son that way," she stated. "Quietly. Without spectacle."

Isha nodded. She had understood this before, but the knowledge was different now—settled, unarguable.

"Vikram was sent away early," Naina added.

"Yes," Isha said.

Naina continued, "The Diwans arranged his education from the beginning. Obligation, not charity."

"They always did," Isha replied.

"Yes," Naina said.

"Until Thapar stole everything."

She paused, and the long-buried history settled into words.

During those three years while Naina lay unmoving, Mr. Diwan discovered that Mr. Thapar had been embezzling business funds. When confronted, Thapar cried, apologized, and begged for forgiveness, promising to repay every rupee. Then he waited.

Using the power of attorney signed in trust, he transferred ownership, drained accounts, and seized total control. Diwan's estate became Thapar's. The betrayal was absolute. Mr. Diwan suffered a massive heart attack shortly afterward and died.

Isha's fingers tightened on the railing. For a moment, she smelled antiseptic again—cheap disinfectant, old cloth, and fear. The kind that never left your clothes.

With nothing left, Isha and her mother were forced into the very house that had destroyed them. Isha's mother was reduced to a maid in the Thapar estate.

Isha remembered her mother standing in the courtyard, head lowered, sari damp from scrubbing stone that never stayed clean. Riya's laughter had floated above it—careless, bored, and cruel.

Mr. Thapar was systematic and unrestrained in his cruelty. He exploited her repeatedly until guilt and despair shattered her mind. She was sent to a mental institution, where she died forgotten, broken, erased.

Isha swallowed. Her throat burned, as if the words had scraped something raw on their way down. Isha witnessed everything. She had learned something then: silence could be louder than screams. And patience, far more dangerous than anger.

In the silence between grief and rage, she made a vow: the Thapars would be destroyed. Not loudly. Not quickly. But completely.

Riya's rise continued unchecked. She humiliated Isha and kept her as a servant. She began slowly poisoning her own father, determined to remove every restraint from her life. Panic attacks weakened Mr. Thapar until one day, he died. She did not think of it as murder. She thought of it as removal.

Riya inherited everything. With no authority left to stop her, she descended into drugs, paranoia, and cruelty. She believed happiness belonged only to her and that anything others possessed had been stolen from her by right. The silence returned, not empty, but resolved.

They watched as Himmat Singh walked away into the darker side of the service road until he vanished from sight.

"He never wanted revenge," Isha stated.

"No," Naina said. "He wanted dignity. He intended to take his life without noise."

"The slap," Isha said. "Yes."

"And Vikram?" Isha asked, though she already knew the answer.

"Vikram understood what his father never needed to," Naina commented.

"That dignity could not be retrieved promptly. Only repositioned." Isha leaned on the railing. "So he worked around the act."

"He never touched it," Naina continued. "He touched what followed."

"The disappearance." "The paperwork." "The press." "And the notes," Isha continued.

Naina nodded once.

From a distance, Vikram called out, "Madam, shall we go?"

Isha exhaled softly. "Fate really has a sense of humor. Vikram is so smart and so handsome, and still, he's a brother."

Naina glanced at her. "Control yourself," she said quietly. "Besides, he's just a child. Let him be."

Then, unbidden, a memory surfaced.

They were children, summer heat, melting ice cream. Isha had been laughing, careless, a smear of vanilla clinging to her cheek. Naina had leaned in without thinking and brushed it away with her lips, a small, instinctive, childish gesture.

thoughtless, affectionate.

Riya had seen it. She had laughed then, loud and sharp, turning it into a joke, teasing them endlessly afterward. The memory faded.

Naina looked at Isha again. More softly now, she said, "And anyway, you are only mine. Only mine since childhood. If anyone ever tries to take you away from me, I won't spare them."

Isha began to protest. "Oh, I was only"

Naina stopped her with quiet firmness. "Don't say anything."

She leaned in and kissed her. The kiss was deliberate and unrestrained. It carried no hesitation, no apology.

Naina didn't try to hide it. She didn't care who saw, who spoke, or who mocked. Let them look. Let them talk. None of it mattered anymore. Only Isha did. They stood close, the air between them still warm from what had just passed.

Isha studied Naina for a moment longer, as if deciding whether the question belonged here at all. Then she asked softly, almost casually, "Why this name?"

A faint smile touched her lips. "Naina Talwar."

Naina lifted an eyebrow. "Why?"

"Because your tongue and your gaze are sharp," Isha said, tilting her head slightly. "Like a sword."

For once, Naina laughed. Not guarded. Not dry. A real laugh is brief, surprised, and unplanned.

"You think I chose it?" she asked.

She shook her head slowly. "This name wasn't a choice, Isha. It was fate."

Isha's smile faded. She waited.

"The day of my accident," Naina said evenly, "there was another accident. Same city. Same hospital." She paused. "That girl's name was Naina Talwar."

Isha inhaled quietly.

"She was my age. Almost my height. An orphan." Naina looked past the terminal lights, toward the dark road beyond. "Her education was funded by a scholarship sponsored by the Talwar Foundation."

Her voice lowered.

"She was brought into the ICU the same day as me. Severe brain injury. Her face was completely destroyed." A brief silence followed. "She lived for three days."

Then, without emphasis, "She died."

Isha did not interrupt.

"My father needed the world to believe that I hadn't survived," Naina continued. "So he did what powerful men always do. He used his contacts."

She turned back to Isha.

"The dead Naina was declared Tina Desai. And the living Tina Desai became Naina Talwar." Her mouth curved slightly, without humor. "It wasn't easy. Not in a foreign country. But corrupt officers exist everywhere."

Isha closed her eyes for a moment.

"My father spoke to the Talwar Foundation," Naina went on. "Records were altered. Files corrected. I became their beneficiary on paper." She paused. "Even today, our company donates generously to the foundation. Every year."

Silence settled between them—not heavy, not awkward. Complete.

Then Naina looked at Isha again, softer now.

"So," she asked lightly, almost teasing, "do you not like my new name?"

Isha smiled.

"A famous writer once said," she replied, "what's in a name?"

They looked at each other. Then they laughed quietly, together. Not because it was funny. But because it was true.

Naina studied Isha for a moment before speaking again. "Ronnie touched you once, didn't he?"

Isha didn't answer, but her silence was enough.

"You know what's going to happen to Ronnie tonight," Naina continued calmly. "The same thing that happened to that bastard Victor. An overdose. Drugs. In a prison cell."

Isha's breath caught.

"Do you remember Uncle Suleman?" Naina asked suddenly.

"The one with the ice-cream shop?" Isha said.

"Yes," Naina replied. "He's in jail now. Framed in a false case tied to Thapar. His shop was taken from him too."

She paused, then added, "I've already spoken to him. Before dawn, Ronnie's story ends."

Isha closed her eyes briefly.

"And Ashima..." Naina went on, almost gently. "Let her enjoy her pregnancy. At least that much mercy."

Isha looked up. "You know who the father is."

"Ronnie," Isha said.

Naina laughed softly once. Then she raised her hand, forming a V with her fingers. Isha frowned, trying to understand. The realization struck her suddenly. Her eyes widened in fear.

"Victor?"

Naina nodded. Nothing more needed to be said. They laughed afterward, the moment easing between them. Then Naina turned and walked away.

Isha remained where she was, tears gathering silently in her eyes. Naina paused, glanced back once, and lifted a finger in warning: *"Dare you cry again."* She then disappeared after blowing a kiss into the air. Despite her tears, Isha grinned.

47 - The Note

At the security checkpoint, Naina reached into her bag to put away her boarding pass. Her fingers slipped into the inside pocket of her waistcoat and froze.

Something was there. Heavier than it should have been. She adjusted the fabric without looking, almost dismissing the sensation. Almost. Then she stopped. Slowly, she pulled it out.

The diamond necklace slid into her palm—cool, weighty, unmistakable. For a moment, she only stared at it. What unsettled her was not its presence, but how completely she had forgotten it was there.

The memory returned with quiet precision. While Ronnie and Ashima were cleaning the scene, she had slipped the jewelry from Riya's neck and hidden it inside the waistcoat pocket. Insurance. Instinct. Habit.

Naina closed her fingers around the gems and slid the necklace back into the pocket, deeper this time, as if concealment could reduce its gravity. It didn't. Ownership, she understood now, was not possession. It was silence without witnesses.

Wearing the diamond necklace, Naina sat near the window, seatbelt secured, her hands still on her lap.

Her hair slid loose on the seatback. She did not edit it.

The glass reflected her face poorly, shattered by the lights outside.

At this level, everything appeared orderly: rows of clouds, defined paths, and expected arrivals.

Leo was relaxing in his airplane container, traveling in cargo.

Vikram was in economy class.

The separation felt great. Roles had already been allotted.

A flight attendant stopped near her and put a folded paper between her fingers.

Her expression did not alter.

The interaction was fluid and conducted like a service routine. Nothing about it suggested urgency.

Naina waited a moment before opening it.

Cabin noise surged, then quieted again. Someone laughed two rows back. A piece of luggage shifted in the overhead bin.

The aircraft continued onward without deviation.

The message was brief. Exactly. Written without exaggeration or apologies.

remember thirty first december.

Now i Know whAt you've done

Before you close the book, just a note to say

The last truth lies in the postscript.

Author's Note

On the Intimacy of Lies began in a way I could never have anticipated. It was first written for my son, Netik, as an English school project. The assignment was simple: write a short story.

That work was completed on June 3, 2021, during the second wave of the COVID-19 pandemic, a period marked by isolation, uncertainty, and an abrupt slowing of life. With time suddenly available and distractions stripped away, I helped him shape the idea. What began as guidance gradually became a quiet, absorbing meditation of my own.

I wrote a brief story, introduced a few characters, and gave it direction. It was never meant to be more than a classroom exercise. Yet even after submission, the story lingered unfinished, unsettled, and persistent.

Over time, a question returned: what if this small beginning could grow into something larger? As I rewrote and expanded it, I drew from years of reading and viewing that had shaped my thinking. Writers like Agatha Christie taught me the importance of structure, restraint, and misdirection—the understanding that tension depends not on excess but on control: knowing when to reveal and when to withhold. Crime thrillers, especially those built on reversals and delayed interpretation also influenced how I approached sustained uncertainty.

This is my first book, and I wrote it without chasing novelty or imitation. Instead, I applied those lessons in service of a story that feels familiar yet distinct. Over time, the focus shifted from the crime itself to what follows it: the routines, silences, and bureaucratic processes through which truth is shaped, contained, and managed.

What you are reading is the result of that evolution from a small school assignment to a finished work of fiction. The story began modestly, but the questions it raises grew steadily. In that sense, the book mirrors how stories often behave: dormant for long stretches, revealing their full form only later.

I did not write this book to provide answers. I wrote it to explore how secrets are neutralized.

On the Intimacy of Lies is not a traditional whodunit by design. The death of Riya Thapar serves as the trigger, not the conclusion. My interest lies less in violence than in interpretation—how institutions process events, how ambiguity becomes documentation, and how proximity itself can be used to control narrative.

Many crime novels treat truth as something buried, waiting to be uncovered intact. I do not share that view. I see truth as regulated, filtered, reduced, labeled, and released in acceptable forms. By the time it reaches public consciousness, it no longer resembles the original event; it resembles something manageable.

This belief informs the novel's refusal of moral closure. There is no final restoration of order, no single bearer of blame. Files close. Narratives settle. The system continues. That endurance, rather than justice, felt most honest to me.

If the ending unsettles, it is because it denies comfort. It reflects a world where meaning is often the first casualty.

I did not write this book in pursuit of recognition. I wrote it in response to a cultural moment defined by speed and disposability. where memory fades quickly and attention is fleeting. A book resists that motion. It asks for patience. It endures beyond the moment of consumption.

Even when it reaches fewer people, a book reaches them differently—slowly, carefully, and with lasting presence.

I wrote On the Intimacy of Lies to create something that might outlast its moment, something quiet, firm, and capable of speaking long after the surrounding noise has faded.

Postscript

Some endings demand to be explored.

If you have reached this point, you may like to look once more at the ending words of the novel:

Now i Know whAt you've done.

There is a small detail disguised in the statement.

Only three letters are capitalized: N, K, and A.

Together, they create 'NKA' - my initials.

This was deliberate. Designers and creative folks may leave a delicate impression on their work, not to announce themselves, but to acknowledge existence.

I planned the novel to finish the same way it unfolds, through suggestion rather than proclamation.

The tale talks at length about what is recorded, what is concealed, and what persists only for those who are paying attention. That final line relates to the world of work. But the mark within it belongs to the creator.

If you found it on your own, then the book has already done what it was meant to do: entice you to read not only for answers but also for traces.

Thank you for reading.

About The Author

Naveen K. Agarwal was born and raised in Siliguri, West Bengal, with family roots in Khirod, Rajasthan, which he considers his ancestral home. He married in Siliguri and currently resides in Kolkata.

He began his professional journey in a family-run transportation business, where he developed an early understanding of teamwork, accountability, and people management.

Alongside his business career, Naveen has remained deeply engaged in creative and humanitarian pursuits, consistently showing interest in socially conscious and community-focused work.

His creative work spans multiple roles, including event producer, anchor, writer, film critic, and singer. Long before influencer culture became mainstream, he experimented with short-form digital storytelling driven by observation and narrative rather than visibility.

Much of this creative work was developed in collaboration with his son, Netik, producing Vine-style short videos that blended everyday humor with storytelling. He has also written and directed two short films, both receiving critical appreciation for narrative strength and execution.